GERTRUDE, GUMSHOE:
Gunslinger City

ROBIN MERRILL

New Creation Publishing

New Creation Publishing
Madison, Maine

Cover by Taste & See Design
Formatting by PerryElisabethDesign.com

1

"What color do you want?"

"Don't try to manipulate me, young man," Calvin grumbled.

Gertrude elbowed Calvin in the side and gave him a scolding look.

"What?" Calvin said defensively. "Everyone knows they ask about color to try to get you emotionally involved in the sale. I hate being sold to."

"Calvin," Gertrude said, "he's a *salesman*. That's *his job*."

The salesperson's eyes flitted back and forth between the two senior citizens before him. He looked unsure of himself.

Calvin looked at the young man. "Fine. I like gray."

They were standing in front of a long row of Ford F-150 pickups. None of them were gray. The salesman—his nametag read Todd—fingered his collar. It was hot out to be wearing a collared shirt. Gertrude was wearing a short-sleeved, short-legged romper. It was red and white plaid with small pictures of Mickey Mouse scattered all over it.

"We could certainly find you a gray one, sir," Todd tried.

"Well, can I get a discount on black, since you don't have gray?" Calvin asked.

It was a Wednesday afternoon in late July, and it was hotter than a hoochie coochie. Hot *and* humid. Calvin believed that this was the best time to go car shopping: on a Wednesday, just before closing time, at the end of the month, when the weather was unpleasant.

"Sure," Todd said. "Let's go into the air-conditioned office and talk about it."

Calvin looked at Gertrude and smirked. She was simultaneously irritated with him and proud of him. Calvin followed Todd, and Gertrude followed Calvin into the spacious car dealership.

Todd tapped some keys while looking at his computer screen. It annoyed Gertrude that the monitor was facing away from her. What was he looking at? And why couldn't she see it? "What you got there, Todd?" she asked.

"We do have one that matches what you're looking for in ruby red—"

"No," Calvin said firmly. "Too flashy. My insurance would go through the roof. I want black."

"We do have one in black, but that has the leather seats, and you said you didn't want leather."

"Oh, Calvin!" Gertrude cried. "Can we please? The leather seats have butt warmers!"

"How can you be thinking about heated seats in this weather?" Calvin asked.

"We're in Maine, Calvin. Winter is always just around the corner."

"Fine," Calvin relented. "But can I not pay for the leather seats, as I don't want them?"

"Uh, no, sir. I'm afraid I can't do that."

"Well, what can you do?"

Calvin haggled with Todd until nearly seven o'clock and managed to get the price lowered a smidge. As Calvin signed on the dotted lines, Todd looked near tears, but Todd perked up when Calvin said he wanted to skip the final detailing. "It's a new car. How dirty can it be?"

And so, at twenty minutes past seven, Gertrude wrestled her walker into the backseat of a brand-new crew cab. "Careful!" Calvin barked. "Don't scratch anything!"

As she climbed into the front, Calvin fiddled with dials and knobs, seeing which things did what. "This thing is like a spaceship," he muttered. He turned on the air conditioning.

Gertrude turned on the passenger side butt warmer.

Then Calvin pulled his new ten-day plates out onto the main drag of Mattawooptock. Gertrude couldn't believe how high up she felt. *It's like riding in the clouds.*

"Calvin," she began.

"Yes?"

"Are you rich?"

He guffawed. "No, I am not rich. I just worked hard all my life and managed my money responsibly."

She looked around the cavernous new vehicle. "Well, this is mighty impressive. I don't think I've ever been in a buggy this nice. Should we go show Andrea?" Andrea was the newest addition to their unofficial detective agency.

"I'm not really in the mood for socializing."

"You're never in the mood for socializing."

"Neither are you," Calvin said.

"True." They rode silently toward their trailer park home until Gertrude heard sirens coming from behind. "Pull over!" she commanded.

"What? Why?" Calvin said, without pulling over.

"There's a cop behind us. Can't you hear that? Were you speeding?"

"Of course I wasn't speeding." He pulled his new truck onto the shoulder. A Somerset County Sheriff's Department car whizzed by with siren blaring and lights flashing.

"Follow him!" Gertrude cried.

"Gertrude, no."

"Yes! Maybe someone's been murdered!"

As he eased the truck back onto the road, he said, "Gertrude, do you lie awake nights just *hoping* someone gets killed?"

"Of course not. But if someone has been killed, it is my duty ..." She stopped herself. "It is *our* duty to help catch the murderer!"

"I don't think anyone's been murdered, Gertrude. Deputy Hale's probably just trying to get home before his Chinese takeout gets cold."

"I do wish Mattawooptock had a Chinese joint that delivered, and I'm not Hale's biggest fan, but I don't think he would use the siren for that. Here comes another one!" Another cop car pulled out in front of them and headed in the same direction Hale had gone.

"That is curious," Calvin admitted.

"Come on! Let's go check it out."

Calvin drove by the entrance to their trailer park and on toward the site of the action. Two cop cars and an ambulance were parked in front of 99 Kennebec Street—a large-for-Mattawooptock apartment complex that stood right on the bank of the river. The three-story brick building was only twelve years old and looked quite modern nestled among its older neighbors. A large sign out front read, "Coming soon: Vacationland condos! Call 207-555-3938."

"Condos!" Calvin scoffed. "Who would buy a condo in Mattawooptock?"

"Someone who didn't want to pay rent?" Gertrude guessed.

"Let's go check it out," Calvin said, shutting off the engine. "But be discreet."

"I'm always discreet, Calvin."

Hale met them at the door. He was coming out just as they were trying to get in. "Oh no," he said, holding up both hands. "Absolutely not."

"We have information about the case," Gertrude said.

Hale stared at her. "What?"

"Let us in, and we'll tell you."

"No. Tell me now, or I'll put you in handcuffs."

Gertrude crossed her arms. "Quid pro quote," she said.

"What?"

"Quid pro quote," she repeated. "You tell me what you know, and we'll tell you about what we know."

Hale looked at Calvin. "Take her home before I arrest her."

"Come on, Gertrude," Calvin said, gently taking her by the arm.

"No!" Gertrude cried, but allowed Calvin to lead her away. When they were out of earshot, Gertrude said, "Well, we know there's a case."

"Yes, it does appear there is a case, and the expression is quid pro *quo*."

Gertrude looked up at him. "That doesn't even make sense. What's a quo?"

2

Gertrude didn't have the newspaper delivered. But the couple who lived next door, in trailer number five, did. Gertrude had explained to them that she collected newspapers, and so they let her have theirs when they were finished with it.

On Thursday morning, she waited anxiously at her kitchen window, scratching Nor'easter behind her ears, waiting for her neighbors to throw their paper onto their steps. Rain jumped up beside Nor'easter on the counter, apparently jealous of Gertrude's affection, and began to purr. "Oh, Rain," Gertrude cooed, "you never want me to love you unless I'm loving someone else."

Finally, the neighbor's door cracked open, and the paper dropped out. Gertrude was off. In record time, she and her walker toddled next door, grabbed the paper, returned to her trailer, and reclined in her only living room chair—though she couldn't recline all the way, as there was a ping-pong table wedged behind her chair. Sunshine jumped into her lap and curled into a ball. "Might get too hot for snuggles today, Sunny," Gertrude muttered.

She didn't even have to open the paper. The story had made the front page. There had been a brutal murder at 99 Kennebec Street. "I knew it," she exclaimed loudly. Sunshine opened one eye and looked at her, but then closed it again.

As she read the article, she became more and more frustrated that she hadn't been allowed to view the crime scene. "So many clues have probably been missed," she said to no one. The article didn't provide much information. Thirty-two-year-old Bethany

Simon had been found dead in her apartment. She had been struck with a hammer. Police were asking anyone with any information to come forward. Gertrude chuckled sardonically. "I had information, and he wouldn't hear it," she said, even though she really hadn't had any information at all.

Her cell rang, startling her. It was Calvin, asking if she had the paper yet. Yes, he'd seen it on the morning news, and no, the paper didn't have any more relevant details. "Want to take a ride over there?" Gertrude asked. "I don't think Hale will still be hanging around."

"No, but I bet the crime scene tape is."

"So? We just tear it down."

"I've got a better idea. Want to go for a ride to Jackson?"

"Jackson?" Gertrude cried in surprise. First of all, *Calvin* never asked *her* to go anywhere. It was always the other way around. Second of all, Jackson was *way up north*. "That's at least an hour and a half drive! We'll practically be in Canada!"

"It is a haul," Calvin admitted, "but I have a good reason to go."

"Has someone been killed in Jackson?"

"Oh, Gertrude, will you let it go? Nobody has been killed. I received an invitation from Gunslinger City."

"Gunslinger City? What in tarnation is that?"

"It *was* an amusement park. Now I'm not sure what it is."

"An *amusement park*?" Gertrude was skeptical. "In Jackson? All that's in Jackson is moose!"

"Lots of moose, lots of snowmobiles, and one old amusement park. We used to take Melissa there when she was young. She loved it. I thought it had closed down, but I've just received a letter asking for a contribution to help renovate the place."

"They wrote you to ask you for money?"

"They did."

"And you're considering it?" Gertrude couldn't believe her ears. She didn't consider Calvin to be particularly generous.

"I am considering it. It was a really neat place. Good old-fashioned fun for kids and families. So, you want to go?"

"Sure. When are we leaving?"

"I'll be there in a few minutes."

"Hang on. I'm still in my housecoat." She hung up the phone and heaved herself out of the chair. She'd taken two steps when the phone rang again. She couldn't remember ever getting two phone calls in the same day.

"Hello?"

It was Andrea. "Did you hear the news?"

"I did. We were there, but ole Deputy Hale wouldn't let us near the good stuff."

"The good stuff?"

"Yes. You know. The clues. The weapon. The body."

"Gertrude, sometimes you scare me. So, are we going to investigate?"

"Of course. But right now I've got to get some britches on, because Calvin and I are going to Jackson."

"Jackson!? Why?"

"I don't know. Some fun-park for kids who like guns. Want to come along?"

15

Andrea didn't answer for a few seconds, but then said, "Oh sure. Why not."

3

"Why did you invite Andrea?" Calvin asked for the third time.

"What do you have against Andrea?"

"Nothing. But isn't it a little strange to bring her along? Why would she even want to go?"

Gertrude shrugged. "I don't know, but I'm sweating like a stuck pig. Can we stop at McDonald's and get some milkshakes? I have a coupon."

"Gertrude, I don't think that's how the expression goes … you know what? Never mind. No, we cannot go to McDonald's because there is absolutely no eating in the new truck."

"It wouldn't be *eating*, Calvin. It would be *drinking*."

"Still no."

Gertrude sighed and reached down to turn off the butt warmer.

"You going to give Andrea the front seat?" Calvin asked.

"No way."

Andrea climbed into the back without complaint. "Wow, nice vehicle, Calvin!"

"Thank you," Calvin and Gertrude said in unison.

"So, what is this place, Calvin?" Andrea asked. "A park where the NRA recruits youngsters?"

"What? What are you talking about?"

"I don't know. Gertrude tried to explain—"

"It was ... or is ... an amusement park for kids and families. The park is set up like a street in the Wild West. There's a saloon, a blacksmith, a bank, a general store, a sheriff's office, even a church."

"Interesting how he thinks of the saloon first and the church last," Gertrude said.

"And they had actors there who would perform these skits." Calvin was visibly excited, and the more he talked, the faster the words came out. "Shoot-outs right in the street. Lawmen chasing bank robbers through the crowds. Women dressed up in fancy gowns—"

"Are you sure you went to this place for your *kid*?" Gertrude asked.

Calvin looked at her. "Of course. What do you mean?"

"Well, it sounds like *you're* the one who had fun there."

"*Everyone* had fun there, Gertrude. You'll see. You could go into the store and buy things in bulk, just like the old days. Or you could buy candy for a penny. Beautiful horses up and down the street—"

"They let you ride horses?" Gertrude asked, her interest finally piqued.

"Well, no, I don't think so. People were riding them, but I think it was just the actors."

"Oh," Gertrude said.

"But, Calvin," Andrea said, "you said it was an *amusement* park. Doesn't an amusement

19

park, by definition, have to have rides and stuff?"

"I don't know," Calvin said tersely. "Maybe it's a theme park, technically."

"Technically," Andrea said, "a *theme* park also has rides."

"Well, you could ride in the stagecoach. Or in a wagon. I'm telling you, it's a great place. I'm not going to argue about it, and I don't need to defend it."

An hour later, they learned that there was plenty to defend. Their first clue was the dusty, empty parking lot. "Well, it's a weekday, so business is slow," Calvin said.

All they could see from the parking lot was a giant yellow wall—several hundred feet long and at least two stories high. There were no windows, and only one entrance. A giant sign read "Gunslinger City." The first "n" was missing. "Goo-slinger," Gertrude said, barely keeping the cackle out of her voice.

They slowly slid out of the shiny, new truck. "This buggy is certainly high up off the ground," Gertrude said with a grunt.

"It will serve us well if we ever have to chase a suspect on back roads," Calvin said.

Gertrude looked at him in surprise. "You've never willingly chased a suspect!"

"I've never had a four-wheel drive truck!" Calvin said as he walked toward the entrance.

Gertrude had never seen him in such good cheer. It was as if years had been shaved off him. She looked at Andrea and shrugged as if to say, "Might as well follow the old nut."

A bell sounded over the door when Calvin opened it. They were immediately greeted by a young man in complete western garb: a long-sleeved shirt (there was no air conditioning, and it was stifling hot in the lobby); a bandana around his neck; and a gun holstered at his side. "Welcome to Gunslinger City!" he cried with excessive exuberance. "My name is Wyatt."

"Howdy!" Calvin cried in delight. "Mr. Earp!"

The man's smile flickered, but then returned to full strength, giving a distinct impression of falsity. "No sir, my name is Wyatt Toothaker. It's my real name."

Andrea chortled. "Well, you're in the right line of work."

"Yes, ma'am," Wyatt said. "I grew up here." He spread out his arms. "My parents built this place, and so they named me accordingly."

"Ah! So you're the one who wrote me the letter? I'm Calvin Crow."

"I am!" Wyatt said, taking a step closer to Calvin and extending his hand. "I sent out letters to people who received our newsletter back in the glory days." He pumped Calvin's hand up and down. "We are working very hard to return to that glory. I think it's more important than ever to offer families good, clean fun."

"Your location could use some work," Andrea said.

Wyatt's fake smile held on. "Yes, ma'am, but I can't really control that. We do get some traffic, from those going to and from Canada, and we'd sure like it a bunch if they'd stop in here a little more often."

There was an awkward pause. Calvin filled it. "So in your letter, you offered a tour?"

"I did! I did! Right this way, my friends." Wyatt headed toward a door on the other side of the room.

"The old city sounds mighty quiet today," Calvin said.

Gertrude noticed a giant fake spider web suspended from the ceiling in the corner of the room. In the middle of it sat an obviously fake, but still menacing-looking spider. It seemed to be sneering at her. She sneered back.

Wyatt opened the door for them, and they stepped through the door of a time machine, one that instantly transported them into a dilapidated ghost town. Calvin gasped.

Gertrude scowled. *What on earth?* They were in the Wild West all right. The *empty* Wild West.

"Where are all the people?" Calvin asked.

"Well, we've had to cut back. I'm assuming you mean the actors?"

Calvin nodded.

"Yeah, we haven't had them for a few years now. We just couldn't afford to keep them on."

Calvin stared at him. "But they were the whole *point*." He looked around the empty city. "I mean, what do kids *do* now?"

"Well, they like to get their pictures taken in the stockades," Wyatt said, crossing the street toward the city center. A small wooden structure offered two head holes and four corresponding hand holes. Wyatt pointed at it with what appeared to be an attempt at pride.

"Parents let their kids put their heads in that thing?" Andrea muttered.

Wyatt had to have heard her, but he didn't react.

"And?" Calvin asked.

"And they are free to explore. They can run around and look at all the buildings."

"Look *at* the buildings? They can't go *in*?"

The smile finally faded. "Not right now. We are in dire need of repair. That's why we need help from friends like you."

Calvin nodded thoughtfully. "Well, is there anything else you want to show us? Or do you mind if we just look around?"

"Please, by all means, make yourself at home. Let me know if you have any questions." He headed toward what looked like a former pigpen.

"Did they really have pigs?" Andrea said, her upper lip curled.

"They did." Calvin looked nostalgic. He paused to look at a sun-faded plastic cactus. Andrea nudged a plastic tumbleweed with her toe. It rolled a few inches. Gertrude thought probably that was the first tumble it had taken in quite some time. Even breezes no longer visited Gunslinger City.

"I'm sorry, Calvin," Gertrude said, and meant it. She'd never seen him so disappointed. And Calvin was usually disappointed about something.

"I just don't understand what happened," Calvin said.

"Video games happened," Andrea said. "Smart phones. Television. Kids don't read anymore. They don't play. They have no imagination."

Calvin looked longingly at the saloon. "You used to be able to go in there and order sarsaparilla for a quarter. You could sit right on a barstool, and there was a guy playing the piano. He'd even take requests. You'd be sitting there drinking your soda and someone would bust in and challenge someone to a gunfight." He looked at the church. "And you used to be able to go in there and someone would be preaching hellfire and brimstone."

Gertrude didn't know what to say. "Maybe we should go. I think this place is past saving. Like Andrea said, unless they install a video arcade—"

But Calvin wasn't listening. He was cupping his hands on the dirty window of the general store. "My wife used to buy fabric here."

Gertrude started. She'd *never* heard him mention his late wife.

All of a sudden, Calvin let out a bellow. "Ahhh!"

4

Calvin turned around and leaned back against the window, clutching his chest.

Wyatt came running. "I'm so sorry, sir, I should've warned you."

"Warned him about what?" Gertrude cried, hurrying over to the window.

Wyatt arrived out of breath and put a hand on Calvin's shoulder. He immediately shook it off. "You should be ashamed of yourself!" Calvin managed breathlessly.

"I am, I am, sir. I'm so sorry!"

"Will someone tell me what in tarnation is going on?" Gertrude demanded.

Calvin stood up straight and stepped away from the building. "Have a look for yourself."

Gertrude leaned toward the window and squinted. It was difficult to see through the inch of dust, but when the dim room came into focus, she too jumped. "What the—" Sitting just in front of the window was a skeleton covered in spider webs.

"Everyone, please! I can explain!" Wyatt took a deep breath. "We had a fundraiser here for Halloween. We decorated the place and some volunteers dressed up in costume. We invited all the local kids to come trick-or-treating and we gave out candy and admission coupons."

That explains the welcome spider, Gertrude thought.

"It was supposed to attract business," Wyatt said weakly.

"Halloween was almost a year ago," Andrea said matter-of-factly.

"Yes, I know. I'm sorry. Look, I'm usually all alone here, and there's a lot of work to do for just one person. I haven't gotten around to taking down all the decorations …"

Andrea leaned toward the window, and then gasped. "Oh dear."

"So you may not want to look into the windows," Wyatt continued, "as there are other mannequins about. In fact, I ask you, please *don't* look in any of the windows. These buildings are being used for storage, and everything's kind of a mess right now."

Of course, this just made Gertrude *want* to look into the windows. She peered into the general store again. The skeleton hadn't moved. She was a little disappointed. She ambled to the next building and looked inside. Sure enough, a green-faced witch hung from the ceiling, a noose around her neck. Gertrude shuddered. She looked back at Calvin to tell him, but he was still busy chewing out Wyatt for sending him an invitation and then trying to scare him to death.

The last building on that side and end of the street was the bank. She peered inside and could just make out piles of boxes. In front of them sat a clown in a rocking chair. She realized then that someone, probably Wyatt, had placed figures in the windows to block out the heaps of junk behind them. The method worked. No one would want to spend much time trying to see past that clown.

Gertrude drifted across the street to the jail. When she stepped onto the boardwalk, it creaked under her weight. "Well, that's mightily impolite of you," she muttered to the old wood. It gave another creak in response. *Better a creak than a crack*, Gertrude thought.

The outer wall of the jail was wallpapered with faded, weathered wanted posters. Most of the photos featured smiling young children, leading Gertrude to believe this was a service that the Gunslinger City of old had offered— printing tourists' children's faces on wanted posters for only $14.99.

Gertrude leaned over her walker and looked inside the jail. She was delighted to see that this building held two dummies, one right in front of the window, and one farther away, in the jail cell. The closest prop was another boring standard skeleton, though he was wearing a cowboy hat, but the one farther away was more impressive as it looked far more realistic.

It appeared to be a corpse with a bullet hole in his forehead. Gertrude shuddered. It was an ugly sight, but she couldn't seem to look away.

And then she realized why. "Uh ... Wyatt?" she called out, still looking through the window. "You'd better get over here."

The pseudo-cowboy extricated himself from Calvin's long-winded lecture and made his way toward Gertrude. "What?"

She pointed through the window. "You have a dead body in your jail cell."

"Yeah, I told you. There are dead bodies everywhere—"

"No, Wyatt. I'm afraid this one's the real deal."

He leaned on the window and looked inside. Then he moaned. "Oh no! That's Spencer. That's my sister's boyfriend."

5

It took Deputy Hale and his men more than an hour to arrive on the scene, and by then, Gertrude had been all over it.

It took some persuasion, but a pale-faced Wyatt unlocked the jail for her.

"Thank you," Gertrude said. "And don't be too shook up. There's no such thing as bad publicity, they say."

Andrea groaned. "I don't think that applies to murder, Gertrude."

"Sure it does," Gertrude said, stepping into the dark room. "People love this stuff. They'll come from miles around. 'The murdered cowboy,'" she said whimsically.

Wyatt flicked on a light. "This was supposed to be a kids' theme park," he muttered as he stepped in behind her. "Aren't we supposed to not touch anything? This is a crime scene!"

"Don't worry," Gertrude said. "I'm a professional. Were you close to him?"

"Nah," Wyatt said. "I hardly knew him. I think my sister was pretty crazy about him, though."

"How long had they been courting?" Gertrude asked.

"*Courting?* I have no idea," he said, and his tone said he didn't care either.

The jail was a mess. An inch of dust lay over everything, and Gertrude began sneezing as she explored the room. There were costumes—sheriff's attire as well as striped prisoner jumpsuits—and props: fake guns, handcuffs, and a solitary harmonica. And there were boxes upon boxes of small plastic stars. "What are these for?" she asked.

"We used to give them out to the kids," Wyatt said sadly. "The sheriff would swear them in and then pin a star on their chests. They ate it up."

"How long's it been?" Calvin asked from the doorway.

"How long has what been?" Wyatt asked.

"Since you did all that."

"Years. We started cutting back seven or eight years ago. Every year we'd lose money, so every year we'd get rid of something, until there was nothing left to get rid of."

"Stop!" Andrea cried. She had just stepped inside the small room.

"What?" Gertrude said.

"The footprints! You're destroying evidence!"

Gertrude looked down at the floor. She'd been so busy looking through the boxes, she hadn't noticed them, but sure enough, there were footprints leading from the door to the jail cell. Gertrude was incensed that Andrea had seen them before she had—*she* was supposed to be the gumshoe after all. "I know, I know," Gertrude said. "I saw them, I saw them! I was going to get to that."

"Then why have you already stepped on half of them?"

"We don't need every footprint," Gertrude snapped. "We only need one."

"That's not true!" Andrea said. "Sherlock reconstructs entire scenes from footprints alone."

"Oh bosh!" Gertrude said. "I've seen every single episode, and Sherlock never does that."

Andrea looked at Calvin. "Is she serious?"

Calvin shrugged.

"What?" Gertrude said.

"Gertrude, you do know that the show is based on the *books*, right?"

Gertrude swallowed. "Sure. I knew that." She looked down at the footprints. "Anyway, looks like a *lot* of footprints for a building that's been locked up since Halloween."

"Maybe we should leave," Wyatt tried. "We've already messed something up. We're going to get in trouble."

Gertrude ignored him and squatted down to take a look. "Most of these footprints appear to be the same size. Maybe even the same boot? But then occasionally"—she pointed to one example—"there's a tiny footprint."

"A kid?" Andrea said.

"I don't think so," Gertrude said. "But a grownup with tiny feet at least." Still half-squatting, she crouch-walked toward the deceased, following the footsteps.

"You are obscuring all the evidence, Gertrude!" Andrea tried.

Gertrude ignored her. "Whoa! Major dustup over here—literally." She sneezed again.

"What is it?" Calvin said.

"Lots of footprints here in the corner of the cell, like someone did some wrastling." She stood up. "And this bench has no dust on it. Something was here," she said thoughtfully. She crossed the small cell to the body and got down on her hands and knees.

"This fella has giant feet," she said. "I don't think he's responsible for most of those footprints." As she peered at his feet, she saw something white behind them. Careful not to disturb him, or the dust on the floor, she reached around his leg to grab it.

No one saw her do this. The item was a pill. She looked it over, decided she had no idea what kind of pill it was, and then slipped it into the pocket of her skort. Then she returned to a squat to look at the gun in the man's hand. "Pretty pathetic job of faking a suicide," she said.

"What?" Wyatt and Calvin said, in unison.

"The killer put the gun in his hand. I'm assuming in an attempt to make us believe that this poor man shot himself in the forehead."

Wyatt took several steps closer.

"The footprints!" Andrea cried.

"I didn't realize the gun was there," Wyatt said.

"We couldn't see it from the door," Gertrude said. "And notice he doesn't *really* look like he's sitting there on purpose?"

"Yeah, well, he's dead," Wyatt said.

"No, I mean, it looks like he sort of fell into that spot. Not like he sat down to shoot himself. And who shoots themselves in the forehead? This was not a suicide. It's not even a well-faked suicide. I think we're dealing with a tiny-footed, tiny-brained murderer."

6

"Did you touch the body?"

"Of course not. I didn't just fall off the turnip truck," Gertrude said.

"What?" As Hale stood glaring at her, a man in a forensics shirt approached them.

"The crime scene has been seriously compromised, Hale."

"How so?"

"It appears someone has recently crawled around the floor, obscuring many of the footprints, and leaving fingerprints everywhere. Also, it appears some stuff has been moved out of the cell."

"What stuff?" Hale barked.

"Not sure. It looks like there were boxes on the bench in the cell, and something made a small imprint in the dust by the deceased's feet."

"Thank you," Hale said, nodding the man's dismissal. Then he glared at Gertrude. "Why are you always here? Why are you always in my way? Did you remove things from this crime scene?"

Had Hale been a smidge more polite, Gertrude would have shared her findings with him. As it was, she lied, "Sure didn't."

Hale's face was redder than Gertrude had ever seen it. "I have cause to arrest you this time. You have destroyed evidence. But I'm not going to arrest you because I don't want to deal with you. So go away. Go home!"

"Can't."

"What? Why?"

"Because we are guests of Wyatt Toothaker. We are here to help him get this place up and running again."

Hale appeared to be at a loss for words.

Gertrude felt a touch on her shoulder. She whirled around to see Calvin.

"Come on, Gert. Let's go home." He sounded notably sad.

"We can't leave!" Gertrude said.

"Why?" Now Calvin sounded notably tired.

"Why do you think?"

Calvin chewed on his lower lip. "Fine. Let's go talk to Wyatt." They returned to the lobby, and Calvin called out Wyatt's name.

"In here!" Wyatt called back.

Calvin followed the sound into a small office off the side of the lobby. Wyatt was on the phone. "No, no, it's not good. It's probably the nail in the coffin, so to speak. But it's the hand we've been dealt. Might as well stop denying it. OK, OK, yep, love you too." He hung up and looked at them. "My mom," he explained.

"Your mother's still with us?" Calvin asked.

"Both my parents are, but my father's not well."

"I'm sorry to hear that," Calvin said in a gentle tone Gertrude liked to call his "grandpa voice."

"Me too. That's what I was just talking to Mom about. Going to try to spare him from this. Hoping the police don't need to talk to him. This will break his heart."

"He really loved Spencer?" Gertrude said.

"No. He really loved Gunslinger City."

The bell over the park entrance dinged and all three of them looked toward its sound. "Do you think that was Andrea leaving?" Gertrude asked Calvin.

"Wyatt!" an angry female voice called out.

The sound of it appeared to pain Wyatt. "That's not Andrea," he said. Then a little louder, "In here!"

A woman appeared in the doorway. Gertrude put her in her early twenties. Her form-fitting dress was stylish if not flattering to her pear shape, and her makeup was flawless.

"Is that Grace Space on your face?" Gertrude asked.

"What?" The woman spared her a disgusted glance and then returned her glare to Wyatt. "Why are the cops here?"

Wyatt tried to make a polite introduction. "Mr. Crow, Ms. ..."

"I'm Gertrude, Gumshoe," Gertrude supplied.

"Um, OK, well, this is my sister, Cassidy."

"Gertrude," Calvin said, gently putting his hand on her elbow, "we should give them some space."

"Is she the one dating the dead guy?" Gertrude asked, ignoring Calvin's prompt.

"What?" Cassidy looked at Gertrude for just a second and then turned to Wyatt. "What's she talking about?"

"Maybe you should sit down, Cass," Wyatt said.

"Gertrude, we really should go," Calvin tried again.

Gertrude turned to him and tried to whisper, but it came out much too loud. "Stop it. I need to see her reaction here." Then she looked at Cassidy. "Your boyfriend has been murdered."

Cassidy fell into a chair. "Murdered? That's impossible."

Gertrude was satisfied that the shock was genuine. "Yes, murdered. Shot in the head. When did you last see him?"

Wyatt glared at Gertrude. "Do you mind? The police are here. I think they can handle it."

Gertrude ignored him. "When did you last see him?" she repeated.

Cassidy shook her head as if confused. "I don't know. Um … two days ago? No, wait … yesterday."

"And where did you think he's been all this time?" Gertrude asked.

"I thought he went home—"

"Home? Where's home?"

"Portland. We share an apartment in Portland."

"Then what are you doing here?" Gertrude asked.

Cassidy looked at Wyatt.

"Never mind that right now," Wyatt said.

"Well, that's mighty suspicious," Gertrude said.

Wyatt gave her another dirty look. "We are a family who runs a business. Of course there are private matters. Doesn't mean they have anything to do with Spencer's death."

Cassidy let out a cry of grief, making Gertrude think that the cry was a bit delayed. Wyatt knelt before her and took her hand.

"It is my job to gather all the clues and then decide which ones matter," Gertrude said.

Wyatt looked at Gertrude. "Your job? Can we just let the police do it?" Then he looked at Calvin. "Do you mind? Can you get her out of here, please?"

Calvin looked unsure of himself. Then he shrugged. "I can, but, believe it or not, she really is very good at this. You might want to let her help."

"Let her help?" Wyatt cried. "Are you serious?" He looked at Gertrude with disdain. "You can't be serious. What, does she think she's some kind of amateur detective?"

"I'm not an amateur!" Gertrude cried, mispronouncing the last word.

"I rest my case," Wyatt muttered. "Really, Mr. Crow, thank you for coming today, and thank you for trying to help, but you and your friends should go."

"Wyatt, do you take any prescription pills?" Gertrude asked.

7

"What?" Wyatt looked appalled. "What do prescription pills have to do with anything?"

"Do you or don't you?" Gertrude asked.

"None of your business!" Wyatt said.

"Oh for Pete's sake," Gertrude said, "don't be so prideful. This is a murder investigation. Don't tell me what prescriptions they are. Just tell me what they look like."

Wyatt looked at Cassidy. "If you'll excuse me, I'm going to get the real cops." He left the small room, barely giving Gertrude time to get out of his way.

"How rude!" she declared.

"I am begging you," Cassidy said quietly and quickly, "please don't tell the cops you found pills."

Gertrude raised an eyebrow. "How do *you* know I found pills?"

"Oh please, why else would you ask my brother what pills he takes? Will you not tell the cops, please?"

"Why are you worried about this when your boyfriend is dead?" Gertrude asked. "The stash of pills I found might be the secret to catching his killer!"

"You found a *stash* of pills?" Calvin said, looking her over. "Where did you put them?" His eyes rested on her walker pouch.

Gertrude protectively put her hand over the top of it. "Don't you worry about that. They are in a safe place."

"How do you know they are prescription?" Calvin asked. "Couldn't they just be over the counter pills?"

"I don't know," Gertrude said. "But they're too teeny to be Tylenol."

"Shh!" Cassidy hissed. "They're coming. Puh-lease don't tell them! I'll explain later."

Hale entered the room, looked at Gertrude, looked at Cassidy, and then looked at Gertrude again. He stood there silently for a few seconds and then apparently decided not to bother. He turned to Cassidy and stuck out his hand. "I'm Deputy Hale with the Somerset County Sheriff's Department. I'm sorry for your loss."

She took his hand and gave it a brief perfunctory shake. "Thank you," she said tonelessly.

Hale pulled Wyatt's chair away from his desk and sat near Cassidy. "When was the last time you saw Mr. Bharda?"

"Yesterday afternoon. I thought he'd gone home to Portland."

"Did he *say* he was going home to Portland?"

"Not in so many words. But I just assumed because ..." She paused, and Gertrude could tell she was being deceitful.

"What are you not telling us?" Gertrude asked.

"Quiet!" Hale barked without turning around. Then, more softly to Cassidy. "What is it?"

"It's nothing," she said, giving Gertrude a quick glance over Hale's shoulder. "I'm just trying to remember. I had some stuff to finish up here, and I thought he was going home."

"What stuff?" Hale and Gertrude asked simultaneously. Then Hale grimaced, and Gertrude smirked.

"Business stuff," Cassidy said evasively.

"You help with the family business?" Hale asked. "From Portland?"

She looked a little sheepish, giving Wyatt a sideways glance.

"That's interesting," Gertrude said, "because Wyatt here told us he runs the show on his own."

"I do," Wyatt said with a hint of growl.

Cassidy rolled her eyes. "I've been a little busy *going to college*. Now I've graduated. Now I'm trying to help."

Wyatt snorted. "That's what you call it?"

Cassidy glared at him. "Do you mind? My boyfriend just died." She looked at Hale. "Where is Hickok, anyway?"

"Who's Hickok?" Hale and Gertrude asked. Hale looked at her. "Will you please stop that?"

"Our kid brother," Wyatt said. "And he's around. But I haven't seen him today."

Interesting redirect, there, Cassidy, Gertrude thought.

"Hickok?" Calvin asked with an inappropriate amount of delight. "Is that his real name?"

Wyatt nodded distractedly.

Calvin looked at Cassidy. "Oh!" he said, as if it was all suddenly clear. "*Cassidy!* Are you named for Butch or Hopalong?"

Everyone except Cassidy stared at Calvin. She was just staring out the window as if she wished she could escape. "Both, I think."

"Sorry," Calvin said. "My timing shows poor etiquette. I just really love westerns."

"Can I see him?" Cassidy asked, standing up.

"I'm afraid that's not possible right now," Hale said. "You will be able to see him later." He looked at another deputy standing near the door. "Get Miss Toothaker's contact information." Then he looked at Calvin. "Can I speak to you?" He stepped back out into the lobby. Gertrude and Calvin followed. Hale looked at Gertrude as he said to Calvin, "*Alone.*"

Gertrude relented, mostly because she wanted to get out of the hot building. She wandered back toward the crime scene, which was swarming with law enforcement personnel. She could see through the doorway and was surprised to see the body hadn't moved. *Ducky is much faster than that*, she thought, fondly thinking of her favorite fictional medical examiner.

She wandered around to the back of the building and found a trail had been cut through the thick forest. *Well, now isn't that strange?* There was no back door to the jail, but there was a window. She wasn't sure if this meant anything, but she thought it worth remembering. She headed down the trail. It was about six feet wide and had obviously been recently traveled. She didn't know much about ATVs, but she figured some type of sporty buggy had been up and down the path, tramping down the sparse grass.

She followed the trail until she got tired— which took about ten minutes. Then she took a short break. But she knew the trail had to lead somewhere. So she pressed on and walked. And walked. Pausing occasionally to catch her breath and to wipe the sweat from her brow. The trail was fairly flat, but the tennis balls on the bottom of her walker were taking a beating.

An hour and twenty minutes after she found the trail, she had gone almost a half-mile. At this time, her trail spilled out onto what looked like a highway cut through the woods. She looked left, then right, and saw nothing but woods. But this was a major trail. She considered continuing her mission, but decided she didn't know which way to turn and didn't have the energy to guess. So she turned and headed back the way she'd come, only this time in less of a hurry.

Before she could see the backside of the theme park, she thought she heard someone calling her name. She stopped walking to listen. Sure enough, there it was again. "Ger-trude! Ger-trude!"

A man was calling her, and it didn't sound like Calvin. *Something must be wrong*, she thought, and picked up her pace. For thirty seconds. Then she stopped.

"What?" she hollered.

Then she waited.

Soon, two deputies converged on her from opposite directions. "She's fine! We've got her!" One of them hollered over his shoulder.

"Of course I'm fine! What in tarnation is going on?"

A deputy tried to take her elbow. "Ma'am, we thought—"

She ripped her arm away from him. "I don't need your help, and don't call me ma'am. I'm not old!" She continued on the trail, leaving the two officers looking baffled.

When she came around the corner of the pretend-jail-building, she found Calvin. "Gertrude!" he exclaimed and wrapped his arms around her.

She stiffened beneath his embrace. "What?" she mumbled into his shoulder.

He let go of her. "Where did you go? We were worried sick."

Gertrude looked at Andrea, who did, indeed, look worried. Then she looked at Hale, who looked furious. "I'm not so sure *everyone* was worried," she said, "but I'm fine. Really. I was just exploring."

"Exploring the forest? Why?" Andrea asked.

"There's a trail back there. Leads right up to the jail—"

"Of course there's a trail," Hale interrupted from twenty feet away. "This is Jackson. The whole town is one giant web of snowmobile trails. And I'm not real happy that I just wasted manpower searching for you while you were out exploring a snowmobile trail—"

"I didn't tell you to spend your manpower on me!" Gertrude almost shrieked. "I was *fine!*" She looked around, her eyes wide. "Can't a lady go for a walk now and again? What is wrong with you people?" She stormed off dramatically, but after a few steps, she stopped and looked back. "The trail led to a highway cut through the woods. Are snowmobile trails really that wide?"

A deputy she didn't know shook his head slowly. "That was the border."

Gertrude was impressed. She hadn't known the border between Maine and Canada in the middle of nowhere was such a big deal. Everyone was still staring at her, making her uncomfortable. "Calvin, would you start the truck? I could sure use some air conditioning."

8

Gertrude, Andrea, and Calvin sat in the truck cooling off. Gertrude's heart was still beating fast and hard.

"What's the big deal about a snowmobile trail?" Andrea asked.

"A snowmobile trail wouldn't be a big deal," Gertrude explained, sans patience. "But one that dead ends at a murder scene is a bit of a coincidence, don't you think?"

"Sir Arthur Conan Doyle wrote that coincidence is really subtle forces at work, forces we don't understand."

"I don't know who Arthur Doyle is, or why you're calling him sir," Gertrude said, exasperated, "but that has nothing to do with this. Anyway, I think that trail has something to do with our crime." She paused. Then she looked at Calvin, her eyes accusing. "What did Hale want to talk to you about in private?"

"He wanted to know what we are doing at Gunslinger City. He thought it a bit of a *coincidence* to find his least-favorite unlicensed private detective here."

"And he couldn't ask you that with me standing there?"

"You aren't always forthcoming, Gert."

"And what did you tell him?" Gertrude asked.

"The truth. And speaking of forthcoming, what was all that about the pills?"

Gertrude reached into her pocket and pulled out the pill. "I found this under the body."

"Gertrude!" Calvin exclaimed. "You've got to stop doing that! One day Hale might really decide to throw you in jail!"

"Oh bosh," Gertrude said. "Hale won't throw me in the clink. He needs my help. He just won't admit it. Too prideful." She gave a self-righteous sniff.

"Why didn't you tell him about that?"

She slipped the pill back into her pocket. "Because he's a meanieface. And you know who else doesn't seem too friendly?"

"You?" Andrea said from the backseat.

Gertrude ignored her. "Cassidy. That little tart is hiding something."

"That's another reason I think you should tell Hale about the pill," Calvin said. "Because she didn't want you to."

"No," Gertrude said.

"Well, I'm going to go tell him," Calvin said, opening his door.

"Calvin!" Gertrude cried, horrified at the prospect of such a betrayal. "You wouldn't!"

Calvin looked at her. "I have to, Gertrude. This is a *murder.* Someone has been killed. We can't be withholding evidence." He slid out of the truck and slammed the door.

Gertrude looked over her shoulder at Andrea.

"Don't look at me!" Andrea said.

Gertrude grunted. "A lot of help you are. Let's go after him."

Calvin was already talking to Hale when Gertrude and Andrea caught up to him. Hale held his gloved hand out. "Give it to me," he said.

She grudgingly reached into her pocket and handed the pill over.

"And you found this under the body?" He slipped the pill into a plastic evidence bag.

Gertrude nodded.

"And why did you take it?"

"What?"

"Why didn't you just leave it where it was?" Hale asked through clenched teeth.

"I thought it was a clue."

"Turn around and place your hands behind your back," Hale said.

"What?" Gertrude and Calvin cried.

"You are under arrest ..." He kept talking as he signaled to another deputy to handcuff Gertrude.

The deputy gently took one of Gertrude's hands from her walker. "Ow!" she cried. "Don't handcuff me! I can't walk without my walker!"

Hale held up one hand. "That's all right. We don't need to cuff her. Just go put her in the car."

"Deputy, that's not why I told you about the pill!" Calvin said, his face red, his whole body shaking. "I told you in order to *prevent* her arrest!"

"Sorry, sir. I really am sorry for you. But I've given her far too many warnings. I just can't keep letting her get away with it. We're taking her to Skowhegan. You should be able to bail her out in a few hours."

Gertrude was grateful to be able to hear this exchange as she was led away. She wondered if she'd have time to get some food at the jail before Calvin came. She was starving. The deputy helped her into the car and then walked around and got in the driver's seat. He started the car and turned on the fan. Hot air blew at Gertrude's face, sticking her orange bangs to her forehead. She tried to look dignified as she pushed them away.

"This isn't the first time I've been arrested, you know," she said, her chin held high.

"No?" he said, pulling out onto the road.

"Nosirree! I stole a forklift once. But it wasn't really stealing, because I was catching a murderer. Just like this time. I'll solve the murder this time too, as soon as I get out of jail."

"I'm sure you will," he said.

"Thank you for your confidence," she said, and then she laid her head back and promptly fell asleep.

9

Jail wasn't so bad, though they told her she'd
have to wait for dinner before she could eat.
(She'd asked for food immediately upon
arrival.)

When they put her in front of the camera,
she wished she'd taken more time with her
hair that day and tried to fluff it up. This
resulted in half of it standing straight up in the
air, and all the hair on the left side sticking out
perpendicular to her head. The right side of
her hair, which she'd rested on for her
backseat-cop-car nap, remained matted flat to
her head. Still, she gave the camera a giant

grin, causing the woman taking the photo to giggle.

Being fingerprinted was great fun. She'd expected a messy ink pad, but instead they simply rolled each of her fingers across an electronic device. "This here doohickey is like one of them newfangled video games," she exclaimed with delight. When they finished rolling her final finger, she asked, "Did I win?"

The woman, who had less of a funny bone than the cop photographer, said, "If you mean are your prints clean, we don't know yet."

They didn't actually put her in a cell, and Gertrude found this both comforting and disappointing. She hadn't really wanted to be locked in a cage, but she thought maybe it would give her some street cred. Instead, they put her in a large holding area with two other people and a television. If it weren't for the metal cage around the TV, it might have been a hospital waiting room.

Gertrude settled into a hard plastic chair to watch the soap opera. After a few minutes of nonsensical dialogue, she looked at the man across the room. "Sure do wish there was some 5-O on."

He ignored her.

"Or some *Murder, She Wrote*? You know, something realistic?"

He still ignored her.

"What you in for?"

Finally, he looked at her. "Lady, I'm not in the mood."

"Fine," she said, and then mumbled, "be a grump."

Soaps ended and gave way to a news broadcast. Gertrude was thrilled to see both murders had made the news.

In Jackson, 22-year-old Spencer Bharda of Portland had been killed by a single gunshot wound. The Sheriff's Department was asking anyone with any information to come forward. The reporter was actually on site, the camera showing a depressing view of the yellow outer wall of Gunslinger City.

In Mattawooptock, 32-year-old Bethany Simon had been murdered in her own apartment. No mention of asking the public for information this time, which led Gertrude to think that they had at least one suspect. She rubbed at a pain in her chest. Being kept in the dark was causing actual physical discomfort.

A woman in uniform stepped into the room and called her name. Gertrude looked up. "If you'll please come with me, ma'am." The woman turned and opened the door, obviously expecting Gertrude to follow.

"Did Calvin pay my bail?" Gertrude asked, using her walker to pull herself to her feet.

"I don't know, ma'am, but your lawyer's here."

"Lawyer? I don't have a lawyer!"

The corrections officer wordlessly led Gertrude into a small, stuffy room, where a man sat at a metal table. He stood and stuck out his hand. "Hi, Gertrude, I'm Stan Fontaine, your attorney."

Gertrude turned and watched the officer close the door, and then took his hand. "I didn't hire you."

"Your friend Calvin called me. Have a seat, Gertrude."

Gertrude looked around the small room. "Can they see us? Hear what we say?"

He nodded to a camera in the corner of the ceiling. "They can see us. They can't hear us."

"So they say," she said, and sat. "So, what's the plan, Stan?"

He gave a pained smile, as if that wasn't the first time he'd heard that expression. "You're being charged with improper conduct in private investigation—"

"What in tarnation does that mean?"

"It means you were acting as a professional investigator without a license—"

"Don't need no stinkin' license to follow the clues—"

He ignored this protest and continued, "and you're also being charged with falsifying physical evidence."

"I didn't falsify anything!"

"Each of these crimes carries up to 364 days in jail"—Gertrude felt her skin grow cold—"and up to two thousand dollars in fines. More importantly, I think, is the fact that if these charges stick, conducting future business will be all but impossible."

"Business?" Gertrude was confused. She'd never had a business, unless one counted her failed attempt at direct makeup sales.

"Calvin tells me he thinks you're in this private investigation business for the long haul. If these charges stick, you will never be able to get a license."

"I told you! I don't need a lic—"

"Yeah, yeah, yeah." He waved his hand to dismiss such foolery. "I heard you. But you're wrong. You don't get a license to prove you can do something. You get a license so that people can't stop you from doing what you already know how to do."

Gertrude leaned back in her chair. "You're a fan!"

He smirked. "I've seen you in the news. I know that somehow, you seem to have a knack for crime solving. And Calvin speaks very highly of you. Here's what I'd like to do. I know the DA. Let me go to him and propose a deal. I'll depict you as an elderly woman who—"

"I'm not elderly!" she shrieked in protest.

"Let me finish, please. I'm not saying you are. I'm just saying that's how we *depict* you to the DA. I think he'll go for it. I'll explain your side of the situation, that you are new to this professional investigating, and that you promise to pursue licensing to prevent future mistakes."

Gertrude frowned. "Sounds like a hard sell."

"What's a hard sell?"

"How are you going to convince the judge I'm just a dumb old fuddy-duddy?"

A small smile flickered across his face. "Just trust me. I can do it."

"And then what? I get off scot-free?"

His face was deadpan. "I'm going to propose community service."

She thought about that for a second. "Can I serve the community by catching criminals?"

10

Gertrude was released about five minutes before dinner time. She didn't know whether to celebrate or complain, so she did a little of both. "What took you so long?" she asked when she saw Calvin.

"Excuse me? I just sat in an unventilated room with an exceptionally unpleasant bail collector for a very long time. I believe what you meant to say was *thank you*." Despite his obvious annoyance, he opened the door for her.

"Thank you," she managed.

"You're welcome. So, how did things go with Stan?"

"I think he's a little bonkers. Going to go with the crazy-old-lady defense."

"Well, Gert, whatever it takes to keep you out of jail. I don't think you realize it, but you are in real trouble this time. I never thought Hale would actually have you arrested, but he seems to be out for blood." He opened the truck door for her.

"Yep," she said, grunting as she pulled herself into the front seat, leaving Calvin to stow the walker in the back. "Had I known, I *might* not have picked up that particular pill."

"Really?" Calvin's eyes were wide with shock.

"Maybe."

He gave her a resigned look and shut the door. She leaned back and took a deep breath. The new truck was already starting to feel like home. Calvin climbed into the driver's seat. "So I suppose you can't go back to Jackson with me tomorrow?"

"Oh goodie. I was worried I'd have to talk you into it. I can definitely go back. I just can't touch anything or get in Hale's way."

"Really?" Calvin looked skeptical.

"Really."

"Stan said that?"

"Well, no, but—"

"Gert, really, don't compromise your situation here. It's not worth it."

"I'll be fine, Calvin. I promise. Stan didn't say I *couldn't* go. I can control myself. I'll stay out of Hale's way. I don't want to deal with him anyway." She stuck her nose in the air.

"So where to? Home?"

"I'm afraid so. I'd like to go nose around that Mattawooptock scene, but my cats must be starving. I know I am."

"I will take you home, but promise me you'll stay away from Kennebec Street. Being seen there *definitely* won't help your case."

"Fine."

"Fine, what?"

"Fine. I promise. I suppose one murder investigation at a time is enough. And I know Gunslinger City is important to you, so let's help them out of this pickle they're in." Saying the word pickle made her stomach growl. "Will you stop at the gas station so I can grab a pizza?"

"What? No!"

She crossed her arms and looked out the window. "Fine. I just thought, since you've been so nice to me lately, and what with me spending all day doing hard time, the least you could do is buy me a pizza."

"*Buy* you a pizza? I thought you said to stop so *you* could get one?"

"Well, that's what I meant at first. But then you were mean."

Calvin chuckled. "It's not that I don't want to stop so you can get food. It's not even that I'm unwilling to get you a pizza. I said no because gas station pizza is disgusting. You're supposed to buy gas at a gas station, not food. If you were supposed to buy food there, it would be called a food station."

"Stop being a pizza snob! They're only five dollars at the gas station!"

"No, Gertrude." He drove by the gas station. She glared at him. Then she snickered.

"What's so funny?"

"I just had a thought—'Pizza Station' would be a nifty name for a pizza joint."

He shook his head. "I'm going to take you home. Then I'll go get you some real food, and I'll bring it back to you, all right?"

She smiled. "That would be mighty kind of you, Calvin."

"I aim to please."

"No, you don't."

11

Calvin rapped on Gertrude's door at six the next morning. Gertrude tried to ignore it, rolling over and pulling the covers over her and Snow's heads. But Calvin persisted.

"Fine!" Gertrude cried, sitting up. "Just hang on to your britches!" She put on her bathrobe, angering Storm, who had been sleeping peacefully on it, and headed toward the door. "What?" she snapped, yanking the door open.

Calvin started. "Good grief, Gertrude! And you call me a grump. I thought you wanted to go to Jackson!" He was holding two cups of coffee.

"I do," she said, eyeing one of the cups.

He held it out to her. "Then get dressed."

She snatched the cup out of his hand. "But why are you here so early?"

"Because most adults get out of bed in the morning. Now go get ready." He turned to head down her steps.

She grunted and shut the door. Then she went about her morning routine with a little more gumption than usual. As she headed out the door, Blizzard cocked his head to the side as if to question her leaving. "Sorry, Blizzard, I wish I could take you with me, but crime fighting is not for kitties."

Calvin was waiting inside the Ford, with the engine running and the A/C on full blast. Gertrude stowed her walker in the back and then pulled herself into the front.

"That was fast," Calvin said, his tone dripping with sarcasm.

"I can be quite speedy when I want to be," Gertrude said and slammed the door.

"Easy! Try not to break my new truck before I get a thousand miles on it!"

"Won't take long to get a thousand miles on it going back and forth to Jackson every day. Are we picking up Andrea?"

"No. Why do we need to take Andrea everywhere now?"

"Because she's part of our team," Gertrude said.

"We don't have a team. We're not investigating this, remember? We are going to Jackson as potential investors in Gunslinger City. That's all."

"Inves*tor*, inves*tigator*, whatever. Fine. Leave Andrea out."

Gertrude slept all the way to Jackson and awoke as Calvin pulled into the bumpy parking lot of the theme park. "Yikes!" Gertrude said sleepily, raising one stubby arm to the ceiling as they bounced to a stop. She saw a cop car in the parking lot. "Double yikes," she said.

"Just stay quiet, and we should be all right," Calvin said.

The bell dinged to announce their arrival. Wyatt appeared in the lobby. "Oh, hi," he said, as if disappointed it was them. His eyes were red, and he looked pale. "Come on in," he said, returning to the small office.

When Gertrude and Calvin entered, they found Cassidy sitting at the desk and a new man standing in the corner. "This is our brother, Hickok," Wyatt said.

Hickok looked much younger than the others and was handsome in a slick, dangerous way.

"You all are up early," Gertrude said. It was eight o'clock. "What time do you folks open for business?"

"Nine," Wyatt said.

At the same time, Hickok snickered. "Not that there's really any reason to open at all."

Gertrude looked at Hickok. "Do you own a motorcycle?"

"Yes, why?" Hickok asked.

Gertrude shrugged. "You just look like the type. What kind do you have?"

"Night Rod Special. You know bikes?"

"No," Gertrude said.

"You're supposed to be quiet, remember?" Calvin said to her. Then to everyone else, "Gertrude is facing criminal charges for illegal investigating, so she won't be able to help you solve the murder—"

"That's a thing?" Hickok said.

Calvin ignored him. "I, however, would still like to help you restore this park to its former glory, if you would like my help."

Cassidy made a loud *pfft* sound.

Calvin looked at her.

"There never was any *glory*," she said with disdain.

"You'll have to ignore her," Wyatt said. "She wants to sell the whole park to some flatlander developers."

"You don't seem to be too shook up over your boyfriend's death," Gertrude observed.

Cassidy's eyes grew wide. "How dare you? Who do you think you are?"

"I'm Gertrude, Gumshoe, and I would think you'd be a little sadder about someone shooting your beau."

"Gertrude!" Calvin tried.

Wyatt, who didn't look too offended by Gertrude's observation, said, "Cassidy has never been one to show much emotion. I'm sure she's just as sad as you'd expect her to be."

Not so sure about that, Gertrude thought. *She looks like a cold, calculating cookie.* "Cassidy, when the po-po questioned you about Spencer going home, why did you lie?"

"What? I didn't lie."

"Yes, you did. Now tell me why, or I'll tell the cops you're a big fat fibber!"

Cassidy closed her eyes. "I *didn't* lie. Not really. It's just ... I *thought* Spencer had gone home, but he didn't actually tell me what he was doing, because we had an argument."

"About?" Gertrude prodded.

"About this stupid park. Spencer thought I was being a bit too pushy. He thought I should give Wyatt some more time to turn things around."

"Wait," Gertrude said, confused. "Who has the final say on this sale?"

"Their *parents* still own the park, Gertrude," Calvin said.

"Actually," Wyatt said, "they've signed the park over to us. What's stopping her is that we each own equal shares in the park, and the vote is two against one against selling."

"About that," Hickok began.

Every head in the room turned to him expectantly, so only Hickok saw the new person enter the office. "Hi, babe," he said.

As Gertrude turned to look at "babe," she saw Wyatt grimace. Then Gertrude made a disgusted face of her own. "Oh dear," she said. Calvin elbowed her. The female of indeterminate age crossed the room to Hickok and planted her lips on his. The kiss suggested she was of legal drinking age, or at least smoking age, but she looked like a sophomore in high school wearing a lot of makeup and not a lot of clothes—a tube top and Daisy Duke cutoffs. "Those hula hoop earrings are covering more of her than her clothes," Gertrude muttered.

"Excuse me?" the young woman said with what sounded like teen attitude.

"You were saying, Hickok?" Wyatt said through tight lips.

"We can talk about it later," Hickok said.

"No," Wyatt said, his voice rising, "we can talk about it now. This is my life you're messing with."

Hickok stood leaning against a countertop that ran the width of the small room, with his arm around his lady friend. He took a deep breath. "I've changed my mind. I think we should sell, Wyatt."

The girl gasped and looked up at Hickok in shock. "What did you just say?"

"Not now, Becky," Hickok mumbled. Then, "Seriously, Wyatt. Let's just be done with it. It's hopeless."

"It's not hopeless!" Wyatt cried. "The letters are working! Calvin here is interested in investing!"

Cassidy rolled her eyes. "The letters? You mean the ones you sent out to our old newsletter subscribers? Most of whom are dead?"

Gertrude snuck a look at Calvin. He didn't look pleased.

"How many of those letters did you send out?" Cassidy asked.

Wyatt didn't answer her.

"Exactly," Cassidy said. "You bought stamps on credit, and you got one potential investor." She looked at Calvin. "Are you rich, sir?"

"No," Gertrude said. "He just worked hard and managed his money responsibly."

Cassidy looked confused.

"No, I am not rich," Calvin said.

Cassidy looked at Wyatt. "So then one investor will not be enough. Will you just admit it? This ship has sailed. It's over, Wyatt."

"Let's discuss this later, when the investor isn't standing in the room," Wyatt said softly, his face red.

"There's nothing to discuss," Cassidy said. "It's two to one. I'm calling the buyer. That is *if* they're still interested. I'm sure they've heard now about the drugs this snoop found."

"Drugs?" Hickok said. "What drugs?"

"She apparently found some pills near Spencer's body. I asked her not to tell anyone, so that the buyers wouldn't find out, but she just couldn't keep her mouth shut."

"Hey!" Gertrude cried. "I can keep my mouth shut!"

81

Wyatt, ignoring this entire thread of conversation, looked at Hickok. "How did she convince you to sell?"

Hickok shook his head. "She didn't, man. It's just common sense. I'm sorry." He took his girlfriend's hand and led her out of the room. Cassidy followed them.

Wyatt sat in the desk chair and put his head in his hands.

"Who's the buyer?" Gertrude asked.

"Vacationland Developers," he mumbled.

Hmm, that sounds familiar, Gertrude thought.

12

Calvin asked Wyatt to show him the actual numbers. Gertrude, having no interest in such things, wandered outside into the sunshine. As she blinked in the bright light, she saw Hickok and an upset Becky round the corner of the giant yellow wall, presumably heading toward the parking lot. Quickly, she followed.

Ten minutes later, she got to the corner of the wall. She peeked around the corner, and then jerked her head back when she saw them. She peeked again. Hickok stood next to a small cherry-red car that looked brand-new. Becky was leaning on it with her arms crossed. Gertrude heard her say, "He's coming tonight." But that was all Gertrude heard. She tried to stick her ear around the corner to hear better, and she heard, loud and clear, Becky call out, "Can we help you?"

"Yes," Gertrude said, stepping out from her hiding spot and ambling toward them. They didn't move or speak as she closed the gap. "I was wondering why you changed your mind, Hickok?"

Looking annoyed, he stuck one arm out toward the yellow wall. "Have you seen this place?" he asked. "It's a money pit. Why *wouldn't* I want to sell it?"

"Why didn't you want to sell it yesterday?" Gertrude asked.

"What?"

"You just changed your mind, right? So what changed it?"

He glanced down at Becky and then back to Gertrude. "The place has sentimental value, OK? But now that there's been a murder here, we're obviously finished."

"Uh-huh," Gertrude said skeptically. Then she just stood there looking at them.

"Are we done here?" Hickok asked. "We were in the middle of a conversation."

"What do you do for work?" Gertrude asked.

Hickok frowned. "Auto body repair."

"Have the cops questioned you?" Gertrude asked.

"About my work? No."

"No, silly, about the murder."

"Of course," Hickok snapped.

"What about you?" Gertrude said, looking at Becky.

"What about me?"

"Have they questioned you?"

"Why would they question me? I wasn't even here yesterday."

Gertrude stared at her. She appeared to be telling the truth. But there was still something fishy about her. Gertrude just wasn't sure what it was. "What do you know about the snowmobile trail behind the jail?"

Gertrude thought Becky showed a small alarm at this question, but Hickok didn't seem fazed.

"What about it?" Hickok said.

"Did you know it was there?"

"Of course I know it's there. I've lived here all my life."

"But *why* is it there?" Gertrude asked.

"How should I know?" Hickok said.

"Because you've lived here all your life."

Hickok didn't respond to that.

"Do you use it?" she prodded.

"Sometimes."

"When's the last time?"

"Look, lady, I don't know, and I think we're done here. I get that you think you're some kind of detective, but I hear you're in trouble for that, so buzz off, or I'll tell the real cops you're harassing me."

Gertrude gave him the dirtiest look she could muster up and then began to stomp off. She'd only gone a few steps when another thought occurred to her. She stopped and said over her shoulder. "It's just a little suspicious you wouldn't want everyone trying to catch a murderer. Guess you're not too scared of whoever it is." Then she continued stomping toward the main entrance.

It was a long journey. Calvin saw her come in. "Where have you been?"

"Investig …" Gertrude started and then stopped when she saw the uniform behind Calvin. "Investing my energy in exercise," she finished. Then she looked at the cop. "Who are you?"

"Deputy Dunlap, ma'am," he said.

Gertrude hated being called ma'am, but under the circumstances, decided to let it go this time. "And what are you still doing here?"

He smiled pacifyingly, but did not answer her.

"He's been here all morning," Wyatt said, "hoping the murderer is going to show up and turn himself in, I guess."

"Did you spend the night?" she asked the deputy.

He ignored her again.

"No, he didn't," Wyatt said. "Why do you ask?"

Gertrude shrugged. "Just wondering." She looked at Calvin. "Are you two still talking about numbers?"

Calvin shook his head.

"Good. I need to show you something." She left through the door that led into the park, and Calvin dutifully followed. She headed toward the church.

"The numbers aren't going to work," Calvin said sadly.

"Oh yeah?"

"Yeah. It's hopeless. They don't need an investor—they need a miracle."

Gertrude didn't care about this. She got to the church, stopped, and turned toward Calvin. "I'm going to stay here tonight."

"What? Why?"

"Because he's coming tonight."

"Who's coming?"

"I don't know."

Calvin shook his head. "Gertrude, start over. What's going on?"

"I heard Becky, you know, Hickok's little tart, say that someone was coming tonight. It sounded very suspicious. I think they're running pills through this place."

Calvin guffawed. "That was quite a leap, Gert, even for you. How did you come to that conclusion?"

"Think about it. We're right by the border. That girl is a criminal if I ever saw one—"

"Just because she wears short shorts doesn't make her a criminal."

"Yes, it does. *And* I found that pill—"

"Which could have been an aspirin for all we know."

"Oh sure, fella sits down to swallow an aspirin and gets shot. Look, yesterday Hickok didn't want to sell. Today he does. What changed? The cops. That's what. The cops are here sticking their nose into everything. I think Hickok and the dead guy were smuggling pills into or out of Canada, they had some sort of disagreement, and Hickok kills Spencer. Now the game's up."

Calvin looked at her thoughtfully. "I'm not saying it's impossible. But it seems like you're making a lot of leaps."

"The boy drives a seventeen thousand dollar motorcycle, Calvin."

"Since when do you know how much a motorcycle costs?"

"Since I typed it into the box on the Google website."

Calvin gave her a small smile.

"How much do you think an auto body repair guy makes in Jackson, Maine?" she asked.

"In July? Probably not much."

"Exactly. He was making his money with pills. Now he's too scared to keep doing that. So he decides to sell to get his share of the inheritance. But there's someone coming tonight. I imagine to get the drugs. Or give them drugs. I don't know. But I'm going to spend the night in the church. And keep watch."

"And then what? What happens if you see an actual drug deal? You going to run out and thump the drug dealer with your walker?"

Gertrude reached into her walker pouch and pulled out her phone. "No, I'm going to film the evidence with my jitterbug."

"All right, well, we don't have to decide right now."

"Yes, we do."

"Why?"

"Because we need Andrea to bring us some supplies. I'm going to call her right now. I just didn't know if you were going to stay and if you needed supplies too."

"Well, I can't just leave you here."

"Sure you can."

"No, I can't. And where am I going to park the truck? They'll know we never left."

"You just drive down the road a ways, pull the truck off the tar, and then cut back through the woods."

"Cut back through the woods," Calvin repeated. "You make it sound like I'm not an old man."

"I didn't say you had to do it *fast*," Gertrude said. "So, do you need anything from Andrea?"

"I don't think so. You really think she's going to drive all the way up here to bring us supplies?"

"Yes, unless she's too mad at us for leaving her home in the first place." Gertrude dialed her phone. "Hullo? Yes, it's me. I need you to bring me some stuff ... yes, we're here ... no ... we didn't bring you because we needed you to come later with stuff ... yes ... get a pencil ... the rope is in the cabinet beside the fridge ... yes, bring it all ... also, feed my cats while you're there ... and bring me and Calvin toothbrushes. They're under the bathroom sink, but make sure you get them out of the bag of new toothbrushes, not the bag of used ones ... and some flashlights ... those are in the box with the rope ... and two cots ... those are in my bedroom leaning against the wall underneath the Christmas lights ... and some pillows ... and some canned beans and a can opener ... maybe even some corned beef hash and some forks of course ..."

Gertrude hung up the phone and noticed Calvin standing open-mouthed looking toward the park entrance. Gertrude turned to look. It was nine o'clock. And people were pouring in.

"Well, I'll be," Calvin said.

"I told you so," Gertrude said. "Nothing sells tickets like a murder."

13

When Calvin and Gertrude entered the lobby, they found a line of people stretching out into the parking lot. Wyatt glanced up at them when they entered. He was pale with panic.

"Can we help?" Calvin asked.

Wyatt nodded.

"Want me to run the saloon?" Calvin said with childlike hope in his voice.

"We've got nothing in there to serve," Wyatt said distractedly as he counted back change to someone. "Can you run this register? I'd like to go straighten up a bit." He lowered his voice as Calvin stepped around the counter. "Get rid of some of the Halloween stuff."

"I wouldn't do that," Gertrude said, eyeballing the crowd. It was a macabre-looking bunch. Not a smile in sight, which suited Gertrude just fine. She wasn't much of a smiler herself.

Wyatt followed her gaze. Of all the people streaming into the children's theme park, not one of them was a child. "Oh, maybe not."

"Maybe just turn on some lights, so people can see the killer clown and the hanging witch," Gertrude suggested. Many of Gunslinger City's new patrons were dressed in black. Some of them seemed to have invested in black eyeliner stock.

"OK. I'll do that," Wyatt said. He looked at Calvin, his eyes wide with desperation. "So can you do this?"

"Yes," Calvin said, looking insulted, "I can run a cash register."

"Thank you," Wyatt said and took off.

As Calvin tried to figure out how to run the old register, Gertrude slowly followed Wyatt out into the park, to see the majority of the patrons were standing in front of the jail. *Too bad we couldn't open the place up*, she thought, but it was covered in crime scene tape. She watched Deputy Dunlap cross the park, work his way through the crowd, and step up onto the rickety boardwalk. Then he just stopped and stood there. People from the crowd began to ask questions, and Gertrude scooted closer to hear.

"I'm sorry, I can't answer any questions," he said.

"Did you find the murder weapon?" someone called out.

"As I said, I can't say—"

"Did he die instantly?" someone else hollered.

The deputy stood still.

"Do you have any suspects?" Gertrude shouted. The deputy looked in her direction, and she ducked behind her walker so he couldn't see her.

"As I said, I can't—"

"So you *don't* have any suspects?" Gertrude hollered from her crouch. Her face was only inches from a tall man's buttocks. He was wearing orange camouflage shorts. She was glad of his fashion choice. She thought maybe those shorts would help her stay hidden.

"We are questioning everyone involved," the deputy said.

As Gertrude scanned her brain for what else she could ask, someone else asked if he could peek inside, and was told no. Then someone else asked if he could have his picture taken in front of the jail, and this started a long line of picture taking. Several people tried to pose with the deputy, including Mr. Orange Shorts, leaving Gertrude exposed. But the deputy had long forgotten to look for her as he tried to avoid the cameras.

Becky appeared beside Gertrude. "What's going on?"

"People love a good murder."

"That's kind of sick," Becky said.

"Yes, well, people are kind of sick, now aren't they? Did you know Spencer?"

"No, not really," Becky said, still staring at the spectacle before them.

"Have the cops said when he actually died?"

"Yeah, sort of. They asked me where I was Wednesday night, so I guess that's when he was killed."

"You said the cops didn't question you."

"I lied."

"Shocker. And where were you Wednesday night?"

Becky finally looked at her. "Seriously?"

"What?"

"Why should I tell you?"

"You don't have to. I was just making conversation. You know, small talk."

Becky turned her attention back to the photo session. "I was with Hickok, at our apartment. We watched TV and then went to bed."

"What did you watch?"

"I don't know. Something on Netflix."

"What on Netflix?"

"I told you. I don't know."

Gertrude took a different tack. "Where do you and Hickok live?"

"Just up the road."

Gertrude waited for her to be more specific. When she wasn't, Gertrude asked, "And what do you do for work?"

"I'm between jobs right now."

"A-huh," Gertrude said, her eyes narrowed. "I see."

14

Somewhere in Jackson, Hickok did some supply shopping, and then opened the saloon. Gertrude fought through the crowd to get to an open barstool.

People were drinking just as fast as Hickok could pour. He looked miserable. He worked his way down the bar, and when he got to Gertrude, he asked, "Would you like a drink?"

"What do you have?"

He looked annoyed. "Sarsaparilla."

She scrunched up her face. "Do you have anything non-alcoholic?"

"Sarsaparilla is non-alcoholic."

"Oh, well, in that case, sure, I'll have a shot."

He poured the glass. "That will be one dollar."

"You're kidding! For this teeny little thing?!"

"One dollar," Hickok repeated.

She took a sip and then scowled. "This is just root beer!"

"Shh!" he hissed and moved on to the next customer.

Gertrude sat on that barstool a long time, waiting for the crowd to thin. It was turning out to be a scorcher, and people just couldn't get enough ice-cold, no-name-brand soda.

At lunchtime, Calvin strolled in and collapsed on the stool next to her.

"Who's manning the cash register?" Gertrude asked.

"I don't know who she is, but someone Wyatt called in to help. Thank heavens. These old legs couldn't hold me up much longer. The people just keep coming, Gert! I've never seen anything like it."

"Yep. Looks like the problem has taken care of itself. By the way, you owe Hickok a dollar."

Calvin took out his wallet and motioned to the reluctant barkeep, who poured Calvin a shot of soda.

"Don't get excited—it's just root beer," Gertrude whispered.

Calvin drank the soda in one gulp. "Let's go find something to eat."

"Go ahead. I don't want to leave. Been waiting all morning to ask Hickok some questions."

"Well, then ask him," Calvin said. "He's right there."

"I'm waiting for the right moment."

Calvin shook his head. "Fine. I'm going to go find some food. And I don't think any problem has been solved. The excitement will die down, and this place will empty out again. It's sad, but I think it's the truth."

"Doesn't have to be," Gertrude said. "They could just keep this theme going."

Hickok happened to be walking by just then. "You're not suggesting we keep having murders here?"

"Don't be foolish. Of course not. But you make it the Haunted West instead of the Wild

West, and you hire people to dress up and scare people." She looked around. "These folks will eat it up."

Hickok shook his head. "I'm not interested in running a freak show. My parents would never forgive us."

Gertrude shrugged. "Up to you, I suppose."

"Yeah," Hickok said. "It is."

"So, Wild Bill," Gertrude said, provoking a scowl from Hickok, "where were you on Wednesday night?"

He paused wiping down the bar to glare at her. "At home. Why?"

"Doing what?"

"Watching television. What else is there to do in Jackson?"

"And what was on the tube?"

"I dunno. Some baseball game."

"Hickok, are you a drug donkey?"

"What? No! Why don't you get out of here for a while, before I do or say something I regret."

Gertrude looked at Calvin. "Let's go for a walk."

They stepped outside to see the crowd had thinned a little, though there was a long line at the stockades.

"I think you meant drug *mule*," Calvin said.

"Whatever. He just lied."

"About not being a drug donkey?"

"Maybe that too, but he lied about the baseball."

"So you say," Calvin said.

"No, really. His little tart told me they were watching Netflix."

"Oh, Gertrude. Who knows what they were watching? It was two nights ago. I hardly think that makes them murderers."

"I didn't say they were murderers. I said they were donkeys."

"I think, technically, one has to swallow the drugs to be a mule. I think, if these people are moving drugs across the border, that just makes them smugglers, not mules."

"Whatever. If you want to get technical."

Calvin gave up then. "All right. I'm going to go find a cheeseburger."

"You do that. Here comes Andrea. I'll get our camp set up for the night."

"Don't let anyone see you."

"Obviously, Calvin. This isn't my first bugaboo."

Gertrude stopped walking and watched Calvin and Andrea exchange a few words as they passed.

Then Andrea approached Gertrude with wide eyes. "Where did all these people come from?"

"Quebec, I expect," Gertrude said.

Andrea tried to hand Gertrude one of the two giant bags she was carrying.

"How am I supposed to carry that? I have a walker!"

"Sorry. Where do you want this stuff?"

"Shh! Keep your voice down. We're supposed to be sneaky!" Gertrude looked around furtively. "Let's take it back to the lobby for now. I've got to get Wyatt to let me into the church."

"You're going to sleep in the church?"

"That's the plan."

"Well, do you really think you should let Wyatt in on the plan? What if he's the murderer?"

Gertrude looked at Andrea for a second and then reluctantly said, "You've got a point." She looked around. There were still a lot of people, but exactly zero of them seemed to be paying any attention to the two mature ladies standing in the middle of the fake town. "Let's go see if we can break into the church then."

They tried to act casually as they strolled around the back of the church. To Gertrude's delight, the place *did* have a back door. But it was locked. "Good grief this crime fighting is exhausting," Gertrude said. "You wait here. I'll go see if I can find some keys."

15

Gertrude returned to find Andrea sitting on the ground leaning against the old, fake church.

"Holy smokes, Gertrude!" Andrea exclaimed.

Gertrude hadn't just stolen the church key. She'd stolen *all* the keys. Out of her walker pouch she pulled a giant key ring, and two other key chains filled with keys of all sizes. "One of these should fit," she said, stepping up to the door.

"Where did you get all those?"

"I pawed around a bit in Wyatt's office."

"And you stole his car keys and his house keys?"

Gertrude shrugged. "How am I supposed to know which key is which?" The first key didn't work. She tried the second.

Andrea started to get up, but then changed her mind and sat back down. "This could take a while."

It did. But after trying the fifteenth key, Gertrude cried, "Jackpot!"

Andrea picked up the two large bags and followed Gertrude into the stuffy gloom. They let the door swing closed behind them, leaving them in almost total darkness. Gertrude felt the wall for a light switch.

"I wouldn't do that. That's like announcing you're in here."

"I know that," Gertrude snapped, dropping her hand. She was tired of Andrea saying smart things. "Did you get the flashlights?"

"Yes, but I don't know which bag they're in."

"Hang on, my jitterbug has a light." She fumbled with the phone and then shone the light at the top of one of the duffels.

Andrea began to dig. Out came the two pillows, the rope, and several cans of green beans.

"I said baked beans!" Gertrude said. "What are we going to do with canned green beans?"

"You just said 'beans'—and I don't know, eat them?" Andrea said, digging into the second bag. "Ah, here we go," she said, pulling out two flashlights. "I brought some extra batteries too."

Gertrude grabbed one of the outstretched flashlights and flicked it on. Andrea followed suit. They cast their weak beams around the small room, revealing several rows of dusty wooden benches, many of them buried by odds and ends.

"Well, at least there's no dead bodies," Gertrude said.

"You're really going to sleep in here?" Andrea asked. She sounded mortified.

"That's the plan. Want to join me?"

"No thanks."

"All right. Let's get out of here and go look for some more clues."

They stepped back out into the sunlight, and Gertrude stowed her new key collection in her walker pouch. Now she jangled a bit when she walked.

"Where are we going?" Andrea asked, when they'd buttoned up the church.

"First, I'm going to go return these keys. Then I need to talk to the kids some more, but I think I made Hickok mad when I called him a donkey. Maybe we should go after Cassidy next."

But Cassidy was nowhere to be found. They found Wyatt in the general store. The front door was propped open, and a few patrons were milling about. Wyatt was apologizing to a tall, gaunt man for the mess. "So sorry, wasn't planning on opening today, but some people have asked us to."

"Have they really?" Gertrude muttered to Wyatt.

"No, but even if we sell just a few things, it will be worth the embarrassment of this mess," he said, speaking rapidly as another customer approached.

"How much for the shot glasses?" a man with black eyeliner asked.

"Three dollars each," Wyatt said.

The man nodded as if this sounded reasonable, and headed toward the counter, which no one was behind.

"I'll help," Andrea said, and hurried in that direction.

"Don't worry," Gertrude said to Wyatt. "She can handle it. She used to be a librarian."

"Is this skeleton for sale?" a woman called out.

"Thirty dollars!" Wyatt called back.

The woman and her friends started to take the skeleton down from its perch.

The cash register made a loud ping sound, startling Gertrude.

"It's all right," Andrea said, standing up behind the counter. "I just plugged it in."

A line formed in front of Andrea. Gertrude couldn't believe it. "I was just telling Hickok," she said to Wyatt, "that you should turn this place into a haunted town experience. Maybe you could get Stephen King to come do a book signing."

Wyatt actually laughed. "Maybe. Right now I'm just trying to ride this wave." He dumped out a box of snow globes.

"Snow globes!" Gertrude cried in delight. She picked one up. It had a tiny gunslinger inside, complete with cowboy hat and pistols on his hips. "I'm going to need a few of these," she said, and began to dig through her walker pouch for some spare change.

16

Gertrude was getting nervous. It was taking Calvin *forever* to get back. She was buttoned up in the small church, and she couldn't see anything. She was loathe to admit it, but she hadn't picked the best spot for a stakeout—because the windows in the church were all stained glass.

It had still been light outside when she'd first hidden in the church, as Wyatt ushered the last stragglers out of the park. That's when she'd realized her error. If she pressed one eye directly to the glass, she could see what was going on outside, but it was a distorted image. She certainly wasn't going to be able to video anything through these windows. Especially in the dark.

So now, as she stood with one ear to the wall, waiting for the sound of Calvin approaching, she tried to come up with a different plan. When she heard the drug smugglers approaching, she would just try to get audio footage, not video. She would record them talking, and if they didn't say anything to incriminate themselves, she would just have to talk them into it. She'd done it before.

But she couldn't get far with her planning because her mind kept circling back to worrying about Calvin. Oh why hadn't she just told him to go home? She didn't need his help with this!

The waiting might have been easier if the park had been quiet. But it wasn't. Pressed right up against the forest, Gertrude could hear a steady stream of unrecognizable noises. They didn't frighten her, but they did annoy her.

Finally, after what seemed an interminable wait, she heard a raspy, "Let me in!"

She scampered over to the door. "You were supposed to use the secret knock!" she scolded, her tummy flooding with relief at the sight of him.

"Why do I need a secret knock when I can just say, 'Let me in'?" he asked, breathing hard.

"Was it a long walk?" She shut the door behind him.

"Might not have been if I'd gone in a straight line." He pressed her phone into her hand. He'd borrowed it for the trek. "It's been a few years since I've navigated by the stars."

"You didn't need the stars, Calvin," she said. "All you had to do was stay close to the road."

"Fine, next time I'll wait in the cozy church, and you can wander around in the woods."

She grinned, but he couldn't see it. "You mean next time you're going to let *me* drop the truck off?"

"Not funny," he said, and sat down with a grunt. "I can't believe they used to make people sit on these things. Pews are bad enough, but backless wooden benches?"

"It was the Wild West. No one went to church."

"So sort of like the world today? Did you set my cot up?"

"Yessiree, right over there. You go ahead. I'll take the first watch."

He didn't argue. He made a beeline for the makeshift bed and then stretched out on it with a sigh. Then he was quiet, annoying her that he'd left her again after such a short visit. She pulled a box over to the wall adjacent to the jail and sat down to listen. The box made a crunching sound, and she sank several inches. She stood, flicked on the flashlight, and looked in the box. It had been full of lightbulbs. *I'm lucky I didn't cut my hiney.* She found another box, this one full of hymnals, and sat on those instead.

After several minutes of that, she realized she was in danger of dozing off. So she decided to eat something. She turned on a flashlight so she could find some of the food Andrea had brought for them. She wasn't going to touch the green beans, so cold corned beef hash it was. She struggled with the can opener Andrea had brought. She'd had several to choose from in her can opener drawer, and Andrea had chosen one of Gertrude's least favorites. She had the can halfway open when she heard footsteps. Her breath caught. She flipped off the light so she could hear better. Yes. Footsteps. Human ones.

She got up, ran a few steps, and shook Calvin's foot.

"What?" he said, too loudly, sitting up.

"Shh! Someone's coming!"

Someone pounded on the front door of the church. Gertrude panicked, looking to Calvin for direction, but she couldn't see his face.

The pounding came again. "Somerset County Sheriff's Department. Open up."

Oh thank goodness, Gertrude thought. *It's not a murderer—probably.*

"Hide!" Calvin hissed, and Gertrude realized she was in a different kind of danger if the cops found her there. Without thinking, she dove under the closest wooden bench. This put her face in a thick layer of dust, and she tried to suppress a sneeze. She rolled over to get her nose away from the dust and realized, once she was looking up at it, that the bench was not as wide as she was.

It was the worst hiding place in the world. She squeezed her eyes shut as if not being able to see the cop would prevent him from seeing her. She heard the door creak as Calvin opened it.

"Ah!" Calvin cried. "Is it really necessary to shine that directly into my eyes?"

"What are you doing here, sir?"

"Well, I *was* sleeping, till you woke me up."

"Anyone in there with you?"

"No."

"You sure? I saw a light through the window. That's how I knew someone was in here."

"All right."

"So, how were you using a light while you were asleep?"

"It was probably my phone. Lights up when I get a message."

"A-huh," the cop said doubtfully, and Gertrude thanked God it wasn't Hale—he never would buy this line of baloney. "So why are you sleeping here?"

"Because I've been helping the owners. I worked here all day. I live over an hour away and I plan to help again tomorrow. So it made sense to just sleep here. Until you woke me up that is." Calvin actually managed to sound put out. This made Gertrude proud.

"And the Toothakers know you're here?"

"Of course. I don't just go squatting in fake churches without permission."

"All right then. I'm going to check with Wyatt in the morning."

"You do that. Good night, officer." Calvin shut the door and then headed back Gertrude's way, rapped his shin on something, and swore.

"Watch your mouth!" Gertrude whispered loudly.

"Shh!" He stood still and silent for several minutes, and his tension made Gertrude stay where she was on the floor. She was just about to drift off to sleep when he whispered, "Your turn to nap. I'll stand watch."

"All right," she said, getting up with a grunt. "You can have my corned beef hash if you want."

A few minutes later, Calvin shook her cot.

"What?" she said.

"Shh!"

"I didn't say anything!"

"You're snoring!"

"I can't help that!"

"Well, the drug smugglers probably aren't going to approach if they hear a chainsaw in the church."

Gertrude rolled over. "They're probably not going to approach anyway with a cop hanging around outside."

17

When Gertrude awoke the next morning, sunlight streamed through the stained glass, creating a beautiful display of dust dancing in the light. She looked around for Calvin, but he was gone. She sat up and eyed the corned beef hash, but then decided she'd rather go to the restroom.

She met Calvin as she was crossing the pretend street. "I already talked to Wyatt," he said conspiratorially. "We're all set."

"What'd you tell him?"

"The truth."

"What?!" Gertrude cried. "What if he's in on it?"

"Oh for Pete's sake, Wyatt's not in on it. He's no drug smuggler. Just look at him."

"You just like him because he wears spurs."

"Perhaps. You can tell a lot about a man by the boots he wears."

Gertrude rolled her eyes. "I don't understand why no one came. Becky said, 'He's coming tonight.'"

"Maybe he started to come, saw the cop, or heard you snoring, and changed his mind."

"Maybe," Gertrude said thoughtfully, looking around the still park. "Or maybe he was never coming here. She just said he was coming. She didn't say where. Maybe we were in the wrong place."

"Well, I'm not sleeping on a cot again tonight, so if you're going to stake out another spot, you're on your own." He started to walk away.

"Where are you going?"

"I told Wyatt I'd help in the welcome center again."

Gertrude had doubts that there would be anyone to welcome, but she was wrong. It was a Saturday, and if anything, the park was even *busier.* Gertrude couldn't believe it. The people started lining up well before nine o'clock.

Wyatt asked her to run the saloon, and she not-so-politely declined. "Where's Hickok?" she asked.

"He's not here."

"Well, where is he?"

Wyatt looked exasperated. "You know what? I don't care. If this keeps up, I can buy those two out and run this place myself. So let him stay away. Let them all stay away." He seemed to suddenly remember she was standing there. "Are you sure you can't help with the saloon? I'll pay you an hourly wage."

"Sorry, too busy." Gertrude took off before he could ask again.

She traveled all over the park looking for someone to interrogate, but Hickok, Becky, and Cassidy were all missing. Deputy Dunlap looked a little bored standing guard at the front of the jail, so Gertrude approached him. "Ahoy!" she called out from about ten feet away.

He smirked. "I can't let you into the jail, Gertrude."

"Did I ask to go in?" she said, stepping up onto the boardwalk.

"No, but I sensed it was coming."

"You seem a lot friendlier than Hale," she said. "Where's he?"

"He's investigating the Mattawooptock killing."

"Oh yeah? How's that going?"

He gave her a look that said, "You know better."

"Has he figured out the connection between the two murders?"

Dunlap laughed. "There is no connection."

"Oh yeah? Well, I'm feeling generous, so I'll throw you a bone. Who is turning Kennebec Street into condos?"

Dunlap furrowed his brow. "I don't know. What does that have to do with anything?"

"Only that it's the same people trying to buy this park."

"Gertrude, I think that's a stretch. It's just a coincidence."

"Arthur Doyle says coincidence is just scuttle forces at work." Dunlap looked hopelessly confused, and Gertrude decided he wasn't very bright. "Just mark my words. There's a connection. So, did they figure out what the pill was?"

"How do you know about the pill?"

"I know things. What kind of pill was it?"

Dunlap looked uncomfortable.

"Oh come on, you can tell me," she coaxed.

"It was oxy."

"I see. So do you professionals think the death is drug related?"

He looked at her out of the corner of his eye.

"I'll take that as a yes. Any evidence that the victim was involved?"

"The victim is clean as a whistle. It was his first visit here. The sister is never here, let alone her boyfriend."

"Really?" This surprised Gertrude. "So I wonder what he was doing in the jail where they stored the drugs."

"We don't know that anything was stored there."

"Oh please," Gertrude said. "Boxes had been moved shortly before his death." She looked around the park. "*Nothing* in this entire park has been moved recently, except those boxes."

His eyes followed her gaze. "Certainly a lot of movement now."

She nodded. "Yep, there's a lot of looky-loos in this world."

They both saw Hale coming across the park at the same time. "Get out of here," Dunlap whispered with a startled urgency.

Gertrude leapt off the end of the boardwalk and scurried around the corner of the jail, between it and the church. Then she peeked back around the corner to see what Hale was doing. He was still walking toward Dunlap, his head down. If he had spotted Gertrude, it seemed he didn't care. But Gertrude didn't think he'd even seen her. She shook her head. *So unobservant.* She crept along the backside of the buildings and then darted across the end of the park till she got to the far side of the bank, where she stopped for a breather. Then she slipped around the corner of the big yellow wall and found herself in the parking lot.

She wasn't sure what to do next. Then she saw the Night Rod Special. *If that is here, then Hickok is here. And if he's here, then he's not at home.* She tried to act nonchalantly as she strolled toward the bike.

Oh horsefeathers! She'd always wanted to ride a motorcycle, but the key wasn't in the ignition. Then she remembered the stash of keys in Wyatt's office.

Back through the front door she went. Calvin looked incredibly suspicious as soon as he saw her. *Maybe he's getting to know me too well*, she thought. "Have you seen my new snow globes? I seem to have misplaced them," she lied. She sauntered past him and into the small office, but he followed her in.

"I don't think you've been in this room since you acquired the new snow globes," Calvin said.

"No, I think I have. And I think I might have put them …" She blocked his view with her body as she sneakily slid the desk drawer open. She was just about to reach in and grab as many of the keys as she could when Hickok fortuitously entered the office. She slammed the drawer shut.

"Excuse me, I need to use the computer," he said, brushing past the two senior sleuths.

"What for?" Gertrude asked.

Hickok shook his head. "Don't you ever stop?" But he didn't answer her question. She watched him sit at the desk and saw something she didn't like. Not only were Hickok's keys *not* the ones in the desk drawer, they were hanging from his belt loop. *How inconvenient.*

She looked at Calvin, gave him a wink, and then she threw the back of her hand to her forehead, cried out, "Ahhh!" and let her knees fold beneath her. She crumpled to the floor right beside Hickok's chair. He looked down in horror. She reached up with both hands and grabbed at his arm, his chair, the waist of his pants, "Puh-lease," she croaked, "helllllp me …"

Hickok looked at Calvin in horror. "Do something, man!"

"I will!" Calvin said, struggling to kneel beside his stricken friend. "You go get help, and I'll take care of her."

Hickok reached for the phone on the desk. "I'll call 911."

"No!" Gertrude cried, partially sitting up, and then collapsing into Calvin's arms. "No ambulance. I just need my medication. My friend Andrea has it. Go find her."

"OK," Hickok said, and he was out the door.

Gertrude opened her eyes and looked at Calvin.

"Is Andrea even here?" Calvin asked.

"I don't think so, but with her, you never know what to expect." She reached for her walker and pulled herself to her feet.

Calvin wasn't so swift in getting up, but he managed. As he brushed off his slacks, he asked, "You wanna tell me what that was all about?"

"No time," she said. "You're busy saving Gunslinger City. I'll fill you in later."

Clutching the keys in one hand, she peeked out the doorway, looked both ways, saw the coast was clear, and made a beeline for the bike.

18

There were only a few keys to choose from, and the first one she tried fit. Gertrude climbed onto the motorcycle and only then realized there was no place to put her walker. "Sorry, friend," she said softly, "duty calls. I'll be right back."

She looked down at the machine beneath her. There were far more buttons than she'd expected. *I've seen Ponch do this a thousand times. How hard can it be?* She turned the key.

Nothing happened.

She found the horn button and was tempted to press it. She thought that would be great fun, but she decided now was not the time. She saw another button with a little lightning bolt on it. *That looks promising.* She pressed it and vroom! the baby started right up. She grinned and bounced up and down a little. Then she remembered she was pressed for time. She looked for a gas pedal, and didn't see one. *Think. What does Ponch do next? Oh yeah! The handle!* She twisted the throttle, and the engine revved, but she didn't move. She noticed the green neutral light. *Got to get this old girl in gear.* She squinted, thinking hard, and vowing to pay more attention to Ponch next time he got on his bike. She remembered him squeezing with his left hand and pushing with his left foot. She tried that. The bike rolled ahead. "Weeeee!" she cried.

She wobbled a bit, and stuck her legs out to try to stop herself, but her feet didn't reach the ground. Only a bit panicked, she squeezed the brake, and the bike stopped. *It's just like riding a bike*, she told herself. *It is riding a bike.* She closed her eyes and tried again, this time giving it some gas. She lurched ahead, but she stayed upright. *Oh Mylanta, I'm actually doing it.* "Woooo-heeee!" she cried as she puttered across the parking lot.

She didn't slow down or check for traffic before pulling out onto the main road.

There were only a few people on the road, some walking, some driving, but *all* of them stopped to watch Gertrude poke by—still in first gear. The baggy romper she wore whipped in the wind and her short orange hair stood straight up in the breeze. Most startling was the enormous smile on her face. She looked like a short, stubby, possibly crazy clown on a really big bike.

She grudgingly stopped at the first apartment building she came to, rolling the bike to a stop in front of the mailboxes, and learned from the "Toothaker" label that Hickok lived in apartment number four. She rolled the bike around to the back of the building, turned off the engine, climbed off the bike, and then really regretted leaving her walker behind.

She made her way to the building, and then steadied herself on the wall as she crept around to the front. She looked everywhere, but didn't see anyone, so she slowly climbed the stairs to their door.

She peeked in both front windows, but didn't see any movement or any lights on. She decided Becky wasn't home. She fiddled with the keys until she got the right one, and then she entered the quiet apartment.

A cat to her left let out a meow, startling her a little. She scooched to pet its head and coo. "There, there, sweetie. If your parents go to prison, I'll adopt you." She stood and began to look around. Suddenly, there seemed to be an overwhelming number of possible hiding spots. She wished she had Calvin and Andrea to help her, but then she realized if they were there, and they found something, she'd have to share the glory, and she certainly didn't want *that* to happen. She took a deep breath and got to work. Through the drawers she went. Under the bed. In the freezer. In the laundry hamper. Nothing. But then she hit pay dirt. In the toilet tank. Giant wads of cash wrapped up in plastic. She had expected to find drugs, but this was pretty incriminating too. She reached for her phone and then realized with dismay that she had left it in her walker pouch back at the park. *Oh beans!* She looked around the apartment for another phone, but there wasn't one. There was, however, a laptop. She fired it up. Then she used Becky's own email account to email the Somerset County Sheriff's Department. *Becky would like to turn herself in for smuggling. Please, come quick and arrest her.* She'd just shut the laptop and stood up when she heard someone at the front door.

She looked around for somewhere to hide and decided on the closet. She closed the folding door behind her and felt around her neck for her LifeRescue pendant. *Dagnabbit!* She had gotten ready so fast the morning before, she'd never put it on. She vowed to never leave home without it again, and wondered, not for the first time, why the LifeRescue people didn't allow her to have a collection of pendants, so she could always be prepared. She would put one in her walker pouch, one in Calvin's truck ... she heard footsteps and began to pray that it was Calvin or a cop—not someone who wanted to shoot her.

"I know you're here," Becky said.

Shucks! There was a good chance Becky wanted to shoot her.

The cat stopped in front of the door and meowed.

Double shucks.

The cat meowed again.

Becky ripped the closet door open to reveal that she did in fact want to shoot Gertrude. At least, that's the message the gun pointed at Gertrude's chest relayed. Gertrude looked down at the cat. "It's all right, sweetie. I forgive you." Then she noticed Becky's feet. "Those are some tiny tootsies you've got there. What size are those?"

"Out," Becky said through tight lips.

"It's too late. The cops are on their way. Shooting me will only get you in more trouble."

Becky looked as though she believed her. "Out," Becky said again, motioning toward a window behind them.

"Out through the window? Are you bonkers? I'm disabled!"

"Out now or I shoot you here!"

Gertrude weighed her options. Get shot in Hickok's kitchen? Or die trying to climb onto the fire escape? She went for the fresh air option.

It was a struggle, but she'd managed to get one leg and her head out the window when Becky gave her rump an impatient push.

"Get your hands off my fanny!"

"Keep your voice down, or I will shoot you right here!" Becky hissed.

Gertrude got her second leg out the window and stood up straight. "Now what?"

"Now you walk."

"Can't. I need my walker."

Becky poked Gertrude with the gun. "I said *walk*."

19

Gertrude walked. And walked. "Why did you kill Spencer?"

"I didn't."

"You're going to kill me, right? So why not just tell me?"

Becky said nothing for a minute. Then she said, "He was in the wrong place at the wrong time."

"He found your stash of contraband?"

"Something like that."

"What was he doing in the jail?"

"I don't know, and it doesn't really matter now, does it?"

"Not to you, obviously, because you're a psychopath. So you killed him because he accidentally found out you were a criminal? Or was he a gumshoe too?"

"*I* didn't kill him. Hickok did."

No loyalty among short-shorts wearers.

"Spencer was a total square. Would've called the cops on us. Hickok had no choice."

"I think this is far enough," Gertrude said, stopping to lean on a tree.

"I'll say when it's far enough."

"Ah, a power-tripping psychopath. Even better. Does it really matter where you shoot me? Isn't this just as good a place as any?" Gertrude's back was to her abductor, so she misinterpreted the ominous click she heard. She thought maybe her end had come, and began to pray that someone would take care of her cats as well as she had.

But then she heard a voice to accompany the click. "Drop your weapon."

Gertrude spun around, wobbling a little. "Dave?" she cried. "Dave! Is that you?!"

"Keep your voice down," he said, without looking at her.

Becky dropped the gun, and then, using multiple expletives, asked Dave who he was.

"This is Dave!" Gertrude exclaimed, as Dave kicked Becky's gun out of her reach. "He's a spook or something. We're old friends. He's already rescued me once, when I caught"—she looked at Becky pointedly—"*another bad guy.*"

"Will you zip it?" Dave said, sparing Gertrude a glare. Then he returned his attention to Becky. He took her phone out of her back pocket and tossed it off to his side. "Don't turn around. Put your hands behind your back." She did as she was told, and Dave secured her hands with a zip tie. "Sit down," he commanded. She did, and he fastened another zip tie around her ankles, all the while keeping his face turned away from her. "Now just hang out for a bit. Your ride will be here shortly."

Gertrude hobbled over to Becky's phone and picked it up. "Can I have this?"

Dave looked at her, ignoring her question. "Can you get yourself back to where you need to be?"

She nodded earnestly. "I have my hog."

He nodded. "OK then. You never saw me. Understand?"

"I understand, but where did you come from?"

"I was here on an unrelated matter and saw you on the motorcycle. Figured you were about to get yourself killed, *again*."

"Thanks. What unrelated business?"

Dave scowled at her.

"Are you chasing drug smugglers too?"

"No, Gertrude, I don't chase drug smugglers."

"We're not drug smugglers, you idiot," Becky snarled.

"You're not?" Gertrude asked, surprised. "You're just a rich person who keeps her savings in the toilet?"

Dave smirked, which made Gertrude feel quite accomplished.

"If you're not a drug smuggler, why did I find a pill under the body?"

"Everyone takes pills, lady."

"What about her?" Gertrude asked Dave. "What if she tells people about you?"

"She would have much less to tell if you'd kept your mouth shut."

"Sorry," Gertrude said, meaning it. "I forgot you were a secret."

"It shouldn't be a problem," he said, looking at the back of Becky's head. "If she knows what's good for her, she won't tell anyone about me."

"Oh, I won't?" Becky asked.

"Probably not. Because you know that I have connections in the Somerset County Jail, and I have even more connections in the prison in Windham—"

"Oh yeah? How do I know that?"

"Because I just told you. But you can tell people about me if you want. I don't exist, so they'll think you're crazy, that you just don't want to admit an old lady got the jump on you—"

"Hey!" Gertrude cried.

"Or you can just forget I was ever here, and then I don't have to make any phone calls." He turned to walk away.

"Wait!" Gertrude said.

"Goodbye, Gertrude," Dave said, without turning around.

Gertrude took off after him, but she soon lost sight of him, and then she realized she didn't really know which direction to go to get back to the parking lot. She panicked a little and instinctively reached for the missing pendant. She remembered Becky's phone and took it out of her pocket, but it was fingerprint-locked. She decided she really didn't like Becky. She headed back the way she'd come, back toward Becky's finger and its magical print, when she heard sirens. *Finally—the slowpokes!*

20

The sirens grew louder and then stopped. Then Gertrude heard barking. She wasn't really a dog person, but these dogs, she loved. She was tired of the forest and wanted to get back to her walker and Calvin.

She heard Becky cry out, and headed in that direction. A few minutes later, she found Becky face down about twenty feet from where she'd last seen her. "What did you do, try to hop away?" Gertrude asked.

Becky moaned, and then the dogs were on the scene. As was Hale.

Gertrude put her hands up. "I wasn't investigating! I promise! She kidnapped me and dragged me out here to kill me."

Hale looked down at the woman on the ground and then back at Gertrude. "And then what?"

"What do you mean, 'and then what'?"

"I mean, how did she end up on the ground?"

Gertrude looked down at her. "Oh. That. Well ..." Gertrude thought quickly. "I told her a joke, got her laughing, then turned around and kicked the gun out of her hand. It's over there somewhere." Gertrude pointed in the general direction Dave had pushed the gun. "And then I wrastled her and tied her hands and feet together so she couldn't get away."

"And you just happened to be carrying around zip ties?"

"Yes. I collect them."

Hale looked around. "Where's your walker?"

"As usual, the kidnapper didn't let me bring it with me. Kidnappers are so unaccommodating."

Hale looked at Dunlap. "Get her out of my sight." As Gertrude was led away, she heard Hale ask Becky, "So what really happened?"

"Did you gentlemen get Becky's email?" Gertrude asked Dunlap.

"I have no idea."

"Then how did you know to come here?"

"We got an anonymous tip."

"You did?" Gertrude looked up at him in surprise. Then she realized Dave must have called it in.

"Was it you?" Dunlap asked.

"Nosirree."

"Well, Hale is going to think it was. How did you really get that woman tied up?"

"I told you."

"Uh-huh."

She didn't like the skepticism in his voice. Not one bit. "You can tell Hale that there's a bunch of drug money in the back of the toilet. He'd better get to it before Hickok does."

Dunlap spoke into his radio, "Gertrude says there's cash in the toilet tank."

"Copy," Hale said back.

"Why didn't you tell him it was *drug* money?" Gertrude asked.

"Because I don't think it is. These aren't drug smugglers, Gertrude. They're *gun* smugglers. They've been moving automatic weapons into Canada."

"What?!" Gertrude cried. "What do Canadians want with guns?"

Dunlap laughed. "The same thing Americans do, I suppose."

"Huh," Gertrude said thoughtfully. "I thought Canadians weren't the murderin' type."

They finally broke out of the woods and into the backyard of the apartment building. "Which vehicle is yours?" Dunlap asked.

"Huh? Um … can I plead the fifth amendment?"

Dunlap chuckled. "I suppose so. All right then. See you later." He turned to head back into the woods.

"Wait!" Gertrude cried.

He stopped and turned toward her. "Yes?"

"Can you give me a ride back to Gunslinger City?"

He looked around at the vehicles all around them. "You can't drive yourself?"

"I don't have a license."

He put his hands on his hips. "Then how did you get here? You don't expect me to believe you walked?"

"The fifth, remember?"

He shook his head, and headed back her way. "All right. Let's go."

"Have you guys arrested Hickok yet?"

"I don't think so."

Gertrude looked at him in surprise. "So he's just wandering around Gunslinger City loose?"

"We didn't have any reason to arrest him. We just got a call that said an armed woman had taken an elderly woman into the woods at gunpoint."

"I'm not elderly!" Gertrude cried. Dunlap opened the door, and she slid into the car. "I've never gotten to ride in the front of a cop car before!"

As Dunlap slid into the driver's seat, she said, "Can you tell Hale to check his email?

Becky sent him an email admitting to everything."

Dunlap looked indecisive, but then said into the mic, "Gertrude says˜ that the suspect emailed you a confession."

There was no response at first, and then Hale said, "I don't think so."

"Tell him to check his spam folder," Gertrude said.

Dunlap started the car. "No, I'm done being your messenger. You can tell him yourself later." He pulled out into the sparse traffic.

"Aren't you going to turn on your siren?"

"No, why would I?"

"Aren't we going to go arrest Hickok?"

"First of all, *we're* not going to do anything. Second, if *I'm* going to arrest Hickok, do you really think I should announce that I'm coming?"

"Oh," Gertrude said. "I hadn't thought of that. I just wanted to push the siren button."

"Well, sorry, you can't."

"Which one is it?"

"Not going to happen, Gertrude."

21

"Park right there!" Gertrude said, pointing to her walker, which stood alone in the middle of the parking lot. Then, sensing that Dunlap was annoyed, she added, "Please."

He pulled up next to her walker, and she got out of the car as fast as she could so she could lean on it. But she didn't have long to rest, as Dunlap was headed toward the park entrance. She hustled after him.

Both Calvin and Wyatt were in the lobby.

"Where's Hickok?" Dunlap asked.

Wyatt's eyes grew wide. "In the saloon, why?"

"Nothing to worry about," Dunlap said without slowing his stride, "I just need to talk to him."

Gertrude chased after him, beckoning Calvin to follow. Wyatt joined the parade.

Dunlap burst into the saloon, which smelled like a root beer factory. The swinging door banged against Gertrude's walker when it swung shut, and that noise made Hickok look up. Gertrude pushed her way through, with Calvin and Wyatt right behind her, and saw Hickok standing behind the bar like a deer in headlights.

"Please put your hands where I can see them, Mr. Toothaker," Dunlap said levelly.

Mr. Toothaker did not respond.

Someone else did. "Oh, this is so cool!" a man in the back said slowly, as if he had consumed a lot of marijuana recently. "Though, that sheriff outfit looks a little modern."

"Everyone, please exit the room slowly and calmly," Dunlap said. Gertrude and her friends moved to the side to allow for the exodus, never once considering they were supposed to be part of it.

Four people, including the stoner, didn't move and remained seated at their tables. A few people grumbled on their way out. Gertrude heard one woman say, "Don't worry, they'll move the show out to the street. That's why they want us out there."

Dunlap waited until most of the people were out of the room and then approached Hickok warily. "I need you to come with me, sir."

"Why?" Hickok said.

"Just need to ask you a few questions."

"Can't you ask me them here?"

"I'd rather you come with me. Please step out from behind the bar."

Hickok did not step anywhere. He did, however, pull a gun out from under the bar and level it at Dunlap, who instantly drew his.

"Wow, those guns look modern too," the stoner said.

"I've got another idea," Hickok said. "I'm going to walk out of here, and then I'm going to drive away—"

Gertrude snorted. *Apparently he doesn't know his getaway vehicle is back at the homestead.* Everyone ignored her snort. Everyone was staring at Hickok. He began to inch his way down the bar, his eyes not leaving Dunlap's.

"I can't let you do that, Mr. Toothaker," Dunlap said.

"Well," Hickok said, "the only way you can stop me is to shoot me, and you'd better make it a kill shot, because if not, I'm going to shoot you, and I promise you, I will shoot to kill."

The stoner clapped appreciatively. Gertrude flashed back to her experiences with poetry slams, and wished the stoner would snap his fingers instead of clap, as snapping was far less distracting.

"I don't want to have to shoot you," Dunlap said.

Hickok came out from behind the bar, still holding the gun outstretched, and headed toward the swinging doors. "Then don't," Hickok said.

Dunlap took a step back. He looked unsteady, unsure of himself.

"Shoot him in the knee," Gertrude whispered loudly.

"I can't," Dunlap whispered back. "He'll shoot me."

Gertrude looked around wildly. *Where's Dave when you need him*? She wondered if there were any other guns behind the bar, and began to walk that way. Hickok looked away from Dunlap for the first time. "Where are you going?"

"To get some sarsaparilla. I'm thirsty, and the service here is slower than pea soup on a Sunday."

"There aren't any other guns back there," Hickok said.

"Hmmm," Gertrude said, picking up speed— a little—"the fact that you thought to say that suggests it's not true."

"I said stop!" Hickok shouted.

The stoner laughed.

"Shoot him!" Calvin yelled.

Gertrude rounded the end of the bar. Hickok fired the gun. Three of the patrons ducked down behind their tables. Gertrude looked around to see who had been shot. A full four seconds after the shot, the stoner ducked down as well. No one had been shot. Hickok had shot the bar. It occurred to Gertrude that Hickok probably wasn't a stone cold killer. "You didn't shoot Spencer, did you?"

"What? No!" Hickok cried.

"Who's Spencer?" the stoner asked from beneath his table.

"Is that what you want to question me about?" Hickok asked.

"Suddenly regretting being so quick on the draw?" Gertrude asked, still slinking down the back of the bar. She saw the gun. It lay right beside a stack of napkins. Was it loaded? How was she going to distract him so she could reach for it? She looked at Dunlap. "Don't worry, Hickok. You didn't draw for nothing. They know you're a gun smuggler— don't you, Deputy?" It worked. Not only did he look at Dunlap, but he lowered his gun, as Gertrude raised hers.

"Don't shoot him!" Dunlap cried.

"I'll try not to!" Gertrude cried back. The gun was wobbling. She couldn't believe how heavy it was and let go of her walker to hold the gun with both hands. Suddenly, Hickok took off, startling all of them—he brushed past Dunlap and banged through the swinging doors.

The spectators waiting outside erupted in cheers at the sight of him.

"Go, Wild Bill! Go!" the stoner shouted, driving one fist above the table in support.

Dunlap gave chase.

Gertrude tried to follow, but she found it difficult to hold both the gun and the walker. She looked from one to the other trying to choose. There was no room in her bulging walker pouch. Her pockets were too small. The gun was too heavy for her teeth. She had to choose.

She chose the walker. She regrettably put the gun down and left the almost-empty saloon. Only the stoner remained, crouched beneath his table.

By the time Gertrude got outside, both Hickok and Dunlap were nowhere to be seen. "Where'd they go?" she cried.

Calvin pointed to the woods.

Gertrude took off.

"You'll never catch them!" Calvin said.

"Yes, I will! You just watch my dust!"

22

By six o'clock closing time, no one had caught Hickok. The Sheriff's Department and Border Patrol were searching the woods—but there were a lot of woods.

Gertrude had collapsed, exhausted, into Wyatt's office chair. He stood leaning against the counter. Someone had dragged in a few extra chairs and Calvin and Cassidy sat somberly side by side.

"I guess Becky has confessed," Wyatt said.

"Seriously?" Cassidy said. "That was fast. She probably ratted out Hickok to get some sort of deal."

"I don't think so," Wyatt said. "The deputy said that she had emailed a confession before either of them had even been arrested. They found it in the spam folder."

Gertrude laughed gleefully, but everyone ignored her.

"You really had no idea about any of it?" Cassidy asked Wyatt.

"Of course not," Wyatt said. "You really think I would have let him run *guns* through this place?"

"People do crazy things to stay afloat," she muttered.

"Yeah, well I don't commit crimes," he said forcefully, and then more gently, "I didn't think any of us did."

"Has he always been a bad apple," Gertrude asked, "or is this a new development?"

Wyatt shrugged. "I guess I don't really know. I guess I don't really know *him*."

"Well he's always been a little wild—" Cassidy began, and Gertrude snickered. Cassidy looked at her, one eyebrow cocked.

"Sorry," Gertrude said, "but you said *wild.* You know, *Wild* Bill?"

Cassidy rolled her eyes. "As I was saying, he was kind of wild-spirited, but he was never a *criminal.* We're a good family. It's that Becky. I've always said she was a bad influence, and now she's proven me right."

"Maybe, but I can't help but feel it's partly my fault," Wyatt said.

"How could that be possible?" Calvin asked.

"Well, I haven't done a great job of running this place. Hickok was desperate for money, obviously."

"Oh horsefeathers!" Gertrude said. "That's no excuse to turn to a life of crime. Besides, I'm sure you did the best you could. And it doesn't look like you're going to have any trouble keeping this place open now."

"I don't know," Wyatt said, sounding unsure.

"Don't be foolish. Of course you know. You just need to do a makeover. Out with the old, in with the new." She put her hands up as though envisioning a marquee. "Gunslinger City: A True Crime Theme Park for Adults. You could even set up fake mysteries for fake detectives to solve. They'll come by the busload."

Wyatt's eyes lit up. "You know? That's not a half-bad idea."

"It's not," Cassidy admitted, "and it might be our only option now. I don't know if Vacationland will even want to buy this place after all this. Drug rumors, murder, and now guns?"

"What did they want to do with this place, anyway?" Gertrude asked.

"They wanted to turn it into a waterpark resort," Cassidy said wistfully, "and they were willing to fork over the cash for it."

"How much do you know about that outfit?" Gertrude asked.

Cassidy shrugged. "Not much, why?"

"I just can't help but think they're mixed up in this somehow."

Cassidy laughed. "I highly doubt it. They're a huge company, buying up properties all over Maine. If they were into smuggling weapons, I'm certain they wouldn't hire the likes of Becky Leeman."

"That's a good point," Gertrude said.

"Well, Gertrude," Calvin said, standing, "I say it's time to head home." He nodded to Wyatt. "I'm sorry about your brother"—he looked at Cassidy—"and your boyfriend, but I'm glad the business part is looking up. Please keep in touch." He stuck out his hand, but Wyatt stood up and gave him a bear hug.

"I've got to say, when I sent out those letters, I didn't see any of this coming." He had tears in his eyes.

"No," Calvin said, uncomfortably removing himself from Wyatt's embrace, "I don't see how you could have."

Gertrude stood and braced herself for a hug, but none were forthcoming. She cleared her throat and said, "Well, you're welcome."

Wyatt looked surprised.

"You know, for catching the murderer and for breaking up the gun running gang that was using your jail and your snowmobile trails."

"They're not *our* snowmobile trails, but you're right," Wyatt admitted, "we do owe you a thank you."

"How about a discount on future snow globes?" Gertrude asked.

Wyatt smiled. "Deal."

23

Gertrude slept in the next morning, and probably would've slept longer except that Sleet batted her in the nose with his paw. He was hungry, or bored, or both. For whatever reason, Sleet wanted her awake. "There, there," she said in a morning-raspy voice, "I'm up, sweetie pie."

She got out of bed and went about her morning routine. Then she toddled over to Calvin's trailer.

"Come in!" he hollered at her knock. This surprised her. He wasn't usually so willing to let her in.

"Mind if I have a seat on the Chesterfield?" she asked.

"It's not a Chesterfield, and since when do you ask?"

She wasn't sure if that was a yes or a no, so she took a seat.

"Did you hear?" Calvin asked. "They caught Hickok. It was on the morning news. He's saying Becky did it."

"Of course he is."

"The cops seem convinced. News said she was primary suspect. I'm sure he was part of the gun smuggling. But I think she was the killer."

"Well good then. That's all wrapped up neat as a pin. Are you ready to go check out Kennebec Street?"

"Absolutely not," Calvin said quickly. "I'm the one paying for your lawyer, don't forget."

"Right," Gertrude said. The truth was, she had forgotten. She hadn't even thought of her legal predicament once that morning. "Fine."

"I know it's not in your nature to stand down, but I think it's absolutely necessary this time. Jail time is no joke, Gert."

"I said fine. I just don't want to see Vacationland Development get away with it."

"Get away with what?"

"With murder!"

"Oh, Gertrude, I don't think they have anything to do with it."

"It can't be a coincidence, Calvin."

"I'm not saying it is. Cassidy said that they are buying up property all over the state. So it's not that big of a stretch that crimes happened at two properties they were associated with. But we know why one crime happened. Spencer found Hickok's stash of guns. So Becky shot him. That has nothing to do with real estate."

Gertrude chewed on her lip. "So how am I supposed to keep myself occupied until the judge lets me off?"

"I don't know. How did you keep yourself occupied before you became a gumshoe?"

Gertrude shrugged. "I worked on my collections."

"Oh dear."

Three days later, Gertrude was alphabetizing her eight-track collection when Andrea surprised her with a visit.

"What do you want?" Gertrude said.

"I was worried about you. I hadn't heard from you for days, and just wanted to make sure you were OK."

Gertrude held up an eight track. "Joe South, best eight track ever. He was so handsome, especially when he wore paisley. And 'Games People Play'? Best song ever."

"Really? I don't remember that song. Do you have an eight track player?"

"I have three of them, but none of them are working right now. If you ever see one that works, let me know. I'd pay a pretty penny to get one."

"Define a pretty penny."

"Why, I think I could go as high as twenty bucks!"

Andrea looked around the room. "Gertrude, you need to get another chair. Where do your guests sit?"

"I don't get many guests. Here, take my seat. I've got to visit the little girls' room." She got out of the recliner, and Andrea, after looking it over skeptically, sat down in her place. Snow curled around her legs purring.

Gertrude was just coming back down the hallway when there was another knock on the door. "Good grief, when it rains, it pours." She opened the door. The man behind it had bright orange hair and matching orange sneakers. "Hey! I know you!"

"Yes, ma'am," the man said. "May I come in for a moment?"

"I don't see why not." She stepped back to make room for his entrance. "Andrea, this is the paramedic who rescued me after I caught the stripper serial killer."

The man furrowed his brow. "She was a serial killer?"

"No," Andrea said. "She wasn't." She stood up and crossed the room toward him. "Gertrude likes to embellish. And you are?" She stuck out her hand.

The man took it, looking around the room wide-eyed. "I'm Jeb Gentry. Nice to meet you. Wow, you ladies sure do have a lot of stuff."

"Oh no," Andrea said quickly, "I don't live here."

"Oh," Jeb said, obviously not caring who lived there. "So, Gertrude, I need your help."

Gertrude rubbed her hands together. "Oh goody! A case! What do you need? Has someone been kidnapped? Someone killed?"

Jeb looked horrified. "Wow, you get excited about other people's pain."

"It's the nature of the feast," Gertrude said. "Now, what is the case?" The suspense was killing her.

"It's not really a case. I mean, it sort of is. Anyway, could we sit down?"

Andrea snorted. "We? No. You? Sure, there's room for one to sit."

"Never mind," Jeb said. He looked at Gertrude. "I'm sure you've heard about the murder at Kennebec Street?"

"Ooooo, this is even better than I thought. Yes, we've heard."

"Well, what the news isn't saying is that there was a witness."

"Oh?" Gertrude said.

"Yes. Well, the police don't really *know* she was a witness, but she was. She lives in the apartment right beside where the murder took place, and I just know she had to have heard something."

"*Heard* something? So she didn't see anything?"

"No, no way. She didn't see anything. But I've been in that apartment, and there's no way someone could get murdered on the other side of the wall and her not hear anything. Those walls are paper-thin."

"So she's lying?"

"Yes," Jeb said, sounding sad. "She is."

"But why?"

"She just doesn't want to get involved."

Gertrude was annoyed. "She doesn't have much choice if she heard a murder take place. She needs to spill the beans."

"That's where you come in," Jeb said, looking a bit unsure of himself for the first time.

"You want me to thump it out of her?"

He shook his head. "No, but I think, if you just talked to her, you might be able to coax it out of her."

"What? What could I do that the police can't do? I don't even have a gun." She looked at Andrea. "I should really get a gun—"

"No—" Andrea started, but Jeb interrupted.

"You won't need a gun." Jeb sounded impatient. "Force won't work. She is not well, and I don't even think she cares if she lives or dies. I just want you to *talk* to her."

Gertrude let go of her walker and folded her arms across her chest. "I'm not really much of a talker, Jeb."

"Yes, you are," Andrea said.

Gertrude glared at her. "Why are you even here?"

Jeb continued, "Well, Anna, that's her name, like I said, she's not well, and she ... she has a lot of issues. And since you are a bit ... um ... well, *different*, I thought maybe you'd be able to relate to her."

"What in tarnation are you talking about?"

"I don't mean to insult you. You're just a bit eccentric, and you know, you have special needs, and so does she, so I thought maybe she'd rather talk to you than a bunch of male cops. Will you just come with me? Just to meet her? Please?"

"I suppose," Gertrude said. "A case is a case no matter how it finds me." She looked at Andrea. "You coming?"

"Yes!" Andrea said, obviously delighted at the invitation.

Gertrude looked at Jeb. "Can you give us a ride? We'd better not involve Calvin in this. He's my assistant, usually, but he's paying for my lawyer."

Jeb looked confused, but he said, "Sure. I can give you a ride."

"Wait!" Andrea cried.

Gertrude jumped. "What?!"

"What if Deputy Hale's there? You should go incognito."

"What's a cognito?"

"I mean, you should put on a disguise, so that if Hale is there, he won't recognize you."

"Hale's not going to be there," Gertrude said. "The murder happened a week ago. He's not still going to be hanging around."

"I don't know who you guys are talking about exactly," Jeb said, "but the cops are in and out of there all the time."

"Fine," Gertrude said. "What kind of costume did you have in mind?"

Andrea grinned foolishly. "This is going to be great. Sherlock was a master of disguises."

Gertrude frowned. "I only remember once, when he painted a mustache on himself and pretended to be a waiter."

"Not the *show*, Gertrude. The *books!*"

"That's a relief. I thought you were going to paint a mustache on me."

"No, but let's go look at your clothes. See what we can come up with." She headed down the hallway toward Gertrude's bedroom.

Gertrude took off after her, calling, "I've got a wig collection! Hang on!" and leaving Jeb standing alone in her living room, with cats swirling around his feet.

Andrea and Gertrude had so much fun getting her dressed up, they forgot Jeb was waiting, so he startled Gertrude when she reappeared and he gasped in surprise.

She now had long black hair and thick glasses, but more shocking was the fact that she was wearing pants. Normal pants, that fit her. And a normal blouse. And normal shoes.

"You look so ... *normal*," he said.

"I don't know what you mean," she said, fiddling with her waistband, "but these clothes are awfully *tight*. I look like a hussy."

"No, Gertrude," Andrea said coming up behind her. "The clothes aren't tight. You're just used to wearing baggy onesies."

"I do not wear *onesies*, Andrea."

"OK," Jeb interrupted. "Can we get going?"

"One more thing," Andrea said. "Gertrude, you've got to lose the walker."

"What?! Why?"

"It's a dead giveaway. If Hale sees you, even in that spectacular getup, with a walker, he's going to know it's you."

"Fine," Gertrude grumbled, and headed for the door.

"Huh," Andrea muttered. "I thought that would be harder."

The threesome stepped outside. "Where's your ambulance?" Gertrude asked.

"I don't just drive the ambulance around, Gertrude. It's not my personal vehicle."

"Fine," she said, and opened the door to his disappointingly ordinary car.

They didn't see any cops at Kennebec Street, and Gertrude wondered if she'd gotten all dressed up for nothing. She was awfully uncomfortable. The wig was hot and scratchy, she couldn't see through the glasses, and her pants, no matter what Andrea said, were much too snug. "Let's go," she said, using the car door to pull herself out of the car.

They entered the building, and Jeb said, "It's on the third floor. Do you want to use the elevator?"

"Don't be foolish," Gertrude said. "I can climb stairs."

Twenty minutes later, they reached the third floor. Immediately Gertrude saw the crime scene tape stretched across the door to apartment 302. She headed that way.

"Wait, that's not where the witness lives," Jeb said.

"I know that. But let's just go take a look around." She stepped up to the door, ripped down the crime scene tape with one swipe, and turned the doorknob. Of course, it was locked. "Oh for heaven's sake!" she said. She looked at Jeb. "Can you pick a lock?"

"Of course not! Who do you think I am?"

"Well, can you kick the door down?" She looked down at his orange sneakers. "Those look like some door-kicking moccasins if I've ever seen some."

Jeb actually laughed. "No, Gertrude, I'm not kicking the door down."

"Fine, I'll just do it myself, just like everything else." She lowered her shoulder and drove it into the door. The door made a loud crack sound, but didn't open. She backed up several feet and then got a running start.

"Gertrude!" Jeb cried, trying to stop her, but of course, she did not heed his protest.

She slammed into the door, which made a louder crack sound before giving way and spilling Gertrude into the apartment, where she landed on the floor with a mighty crash.

"Ow!" she cried.

Andrea rushed to her side. "Are you all right?"

Gertrude sat up, rubbing her shoulder. "I think so, but if I'm not, at least we've got a paramedic." She painfully picked herself up and looked around the room.

"Your wig's crooked," Andrea said, and reached up to fix it.

Gertrude slapped her hand away. "Stop fiddling with me. All right, this will go faster if you guys help me look."

"What are we looking for?"

"Anything interesting. Large wads of cash, bags of drugs, weapons, snacks."

"Snacks?" Jeb said.

"Yes, smashing through doors has whet my appetite."

Jeb wandered into the kitchen. "I'm pretty sure the cops have already searched this place, Gertrude. I didn't ask you here for your investigative skills; I just wanted you to talk to the witness."

"We'll get to that," Gertrude said.

"Not if we get arrested first," Andrea muttered.

"I'm too hungry to go to jail again," Gertrude admitted.

"Again?" Jeb said.

"So let's make this quick," Gertrude said. "Jeb, check the toilet tank. Andrea, check the freezer." Gertrude started sifting through the paperwork on the victim's desk. "Hey, guys, look! A red herring!"

Andrea came up behind her. "The thing about a red herring is you're not supposed to *know* it's a red herring immediately upon finding it," Andrea said.

Gertrude looked at her, confused. "I don't know what you're talking about, but this *says* it's a red herring. Look." She pointed. A bunch of pages were stapled together and on the cover page was written in red ink: Red Herring. Vacationland Development. Kennebec Street Condos.

"Well isn't that interesting," Andrea said.

"It's a real estate thing," Jeb said. "Anna got one too. This apartment building is going condo, so all the residents got one."

"Going condo?" Gertrude said.

"Yes, they either have to buy their apartments or get out. They were given thirty days."

"Is that even legal?" Andrea asked.

"There was a clause in their leases that said they could be terminated at any time with thirty days' notice, so yes."

"Is Anna moving out?" Gertrude asked.

"I highly doubt it," Jeb said. "Can we go talk to her now?"

"Sure," Gertrude said. She went to shove the document in her walker pouch, but then realized she didn't have it with her. She tried to shove it in the back of her waistband, but it didn't fit. "Andrea," she snapped. "Take this."

Andrea shoved it into her purse, and they headed out into the hallway. Gertrude shut the obviously-broken door and then stuck the crime scene tape back up crooked.

"Right," Jeb said, "they'll never suspect a thing." He walked to the next doorway and knocked.

It was opened immediately.

"Oh, hi, Jeb," a woman said, obviously surprised to see him. She stuck her head out and looked up and down the hallway. "Are you the ones making all the noise next door?"
"Hi, Jackie. These are my friends Gertrude and Andrea. I was hoping we could talk to Anna for a few minutes?"

24

Jackie appeared to be pleased to see Jeb, but when he said, "We'd just like to talk to her about the crime," her expression changed drastically.

Well, isn't that suspicious, Gertrude thought.

"Why do *you* want to talk to her? The cops have already harassed us enough. She didn't hear anything. Why can't people just leave her alone?"

Gertrude stepped forward. "I'm a gumshoe. I specialize in getting people to talk." Then she pushed past Jackie and into her apartment. She looked around but didn't see anyone else there. She turned around. "Is Anna not home?"

Jackie looked at Jeb. "You didn't tell her?"

"Tell me what?"

"Follow me, Gertrude," Jeb said, and crossed the apartment to a door, which he softly knocked on. "Anna? It's Jeb, the paramedic. Can I come in?"

Gertrude didn't hear her answer, but Jeb opened the door anyway.

Gertrude gasped. "Oh my."

The woman's body covered most of the bed she lay on. Her head and enormous shoulders were propped up on several pillows. The woman appeared to be in pain or at least significant discomfort. A television was mounted on the wall, turned to *The Price Is Right*. There was a bathroom to their right, and most of the wall between it and the bedroom had been removed. Gertrude looked at her team. "Give us a minute?"

Jeb nodded, backed out of the room, and shut the door, leaving Gertrude alone with Anna. "Mind if I sit for bit? I'm Gertrude, and I love *The Price Is Right*."

Anna answered with a slight shake of her head.

Gertrude sat in a wing chair beside Anna's bed. "Have you ever noticed the price is never really right? Always seems a bit high to me." She paused. Then, "Are you hurt?"

"No, just fat," Anna said.

Gertrude smiled. "I prefer to use the word *fluffy*."

Anna's lips curled up just a little. "I might be a bit beyond *fluffy*."

"I'm not sure fluffiness is an exact measurement. So I hear you overheard a crime."

Anna shook her head more vehemently. "I didn't hear anything."

"Now, we both know that's not true." Gertrude looked around the room. "You don't leave this room much, do you?"

Another head shake.

"Haven't left it in a while?"

Anna just looked at her.

"And you're afraid that if you say you heard something, you'll have to leave? You'll have to go to court?"

"I'm not afraid of anything," Anna said after a long pause. "I just didn't hear anything."

"Our pal Jeb says these walls are very thin. I could send him over, ask him to holler for a bit, and see if we can hear him?"

Anna looked alarmed. "I must have been asleep when it happened."

"You must be a deep sleeper."

Anna didn't say anything.

"I used to live in an apartment. I used to go for weeks at a time without leaving. The thing was, I didn't really like people. I liked *stuff*. And I liked my cats. Do you have a cat?"

Anna shook her head.

"Oh, you should get one. I could get one for you. They help. A lot. With life and everything." She paused, looking around the small space. "Anna, you don't have to stay in this room. I get why you might want to, but you don't have to."

"I know," Anna said. She was crying now. "But I'm trapped."

Gertrude looked at the doorway and then at Anna's girth. "You don't fit through the door?"

Anna didn't answer.

"Still, there's got to be a way to get you out of here." Some wires connected in Gertrude's brain then. "Are you guys buying this apartment?"

Anna didn't answer.

"So you're going to *have* to leave, right? How much longer?"

"Eight days," Anna said so quietly that Gertrude had to read her lips.

"Do you have a plan?"

Anna shook her head. Her tears flowed faster.

Gertrude leaned forward. "I'm pretty smart, Anna. We're going to figure this out. That's what I do—figure things out."

The look on Anna's face made Gertrude's blood run cold. "No, Anna, that *is not* the answer. How old are you?"

"Twenty-seven."

"All right then. You've got a whole life ahead of you. No need to quit now."

Anna started to blubber. Gertrude closed her eyes, in part to give Anna a little more privacy, and in part to visualize the hallway and the stairwell. "Anna, if we can just get you into the hallway, the rest will be a piece of cake."

"And then what?"

"And then our friend Jeb will get you to the hospital, and you'll start getting better. I promise you, Anna, you can do this. We've all got our hiccups. But we just keep living." Something flickered in Anna's eyes. Gertrude thought it might be hope. "In the meantime, you've got to tell me what you heard."

The hope disappeared. "Is that why you're being so nice to me? Just to get me to tell you what I heard?"

"Aha! So you did hear something. No, Anna, I'm being nice to you because you need someone to be nice to you. And because I can understand how someone could find themselves in such a ... well ... such a hiccup. But there are two different issues here. There's your freedom, and there's a murderer on the loose that you can help catch. But those are two different problems."

"But they're not," Anna blubbered.

"Yes, they are. If you're already getting out of bed, then getting to court months from now isn't such a big deal."

"It's not about court!" Anna snapped.

Gertrude smiled. *Finally. Sounds like there's a little spunk in there after all.*

Someone knocked on the door. Jeb's voice asked, "Everything OK in there?"

"Peachy!" Gertrude hollered. "Now leave us alone!" She looked at Anna, and said more softly, "If it's not about court, then what's it about?"

"I didn't hear anything."

"But you did. You've already admitted it."

Anna closed her eyes, but the tears kept flowing.

Gertrude scooted the chair closer to her bed and put one of her hands on Anna's. "I have to have a walker to walk. I can't go anywhere without it. Except when I have to. Then I can. You can leave this room, Anna."

"Why does any of this matter to you?" Anna said.

"Because Bethany Simon was my niece, and I want to catch her killer."

Horror filled Anna's face. "I'm so sorry. I didn't know. Were you close?"

"Very. She never mentioned me?"

Anna shook her head. "I never actually talked to her."

A thought occurred to Gertrude. "Anna, do you *know* who killed Bethany?" And there it was. She did know. "I'm sorry, Anna. All this time I thought you just knew *something*, not *the whole thing*. It would be easier to share small details than to outright accuse someone of murder, but you've still got to do it. Are you scared of this thug?"

Anna shook her head. "I don't know anything."

"Anna, you can't just let a bad guy walk free."

"But what if it's not a bad guy?"

"It? Did a robot kill her? Oh, wait ... you said *it* to avoid saying *she*, didn't you?"

Anna looked at the television. It was time for Plinko. Gertrude loved Plinko. She tried not to get distracted.

"So you know the killer, and the killer's a she, so the killer is ... Anna, does Jackie live here too?"

A small nod.

"Is she your sister?"

Another small nod.

Gertrude took a deep breath. She wasn't sure, but she pretended she was: "Anna, why did Jackie kill Bethany?"

A fresh onslaught of tears. "You will never be able to get me to say that she did anything."

"All right, all right. Just tell me. She must have had a good reason to do such a thing, right?"

Anna sniffed. "Bethany bought our apartment."

"Oh!" Gertrude said. *That would be a problem.* "But don't you get first dibs, since you live here?"

"Yes, but we couldn't come up with the money. We have a lot of debt, because of all the medical bills. The ambulance has to come all the time, so the bills come faster than

Jackie can pay them. She works all the time, and she told the developers—"

"Vacationland Developers?" Gertrude interrupted.

"Yes, Jackie told them that she would get the money together, but they didn't give her enough time. And then Bethany bought it. Said she was going to knock a wall down and make one big condo."

Gertrude leaned back. "But Anna, that's not a reason to *kill* someone."

"Yes, it is!" she screeched. Then she coughed and said, more quietly, "OK, maybe not, but she didn't know what to do. She can't get me out of here. And we're being forced to leave, and then Bethany said, 'Why doesn't Anna just kill herself? Then you could take her out in pieces.'" Anna's shoulders shook with her sobs. "So Jackie just lost it. She just hit her."

"She just happened to be holding a hammer?"

"No, she went over there to get hers back. Bethany had borrowed it. And then when she was over there, she found out about what

Bethany had done, and well ... well, it just happened."

"That must have been a horrible thing to have to listen to," Gertrude said softly.

"Yes, it was," Anna said, gasping, "and there was nothing I could do to stop it." She put her hands over her face and sobbed.

Gertrude let her cry for a minute, and then said, "Anna, I know you love your sister, but she did a bad thing."

Through her hands, Anna sputtered, "But she's been working so hard all this time, taking care of me every day ... I can't say anything."

The door to the room flew open, and Jackie came running in. "It's OK, Anna, it's OK."

Anna sobbed even harder, which Gertrude didn't think was possible. "No, it's not," she said, blubbering.

Jackie wrapped her arms around Anna. "Yes, it is. I'm so sorry. I didn't know. I really didn't know you heard all that." Gertrude looked at the doorway, where Jeb and Andrea stood looking on. Andrea's eyes were wide, and Jeb's were wet with tears.

Anna let go of Jackie and looked at her. "You just heard what I said to Gertrude?"

"Yes, these walls are thin, remember? But I didn't know you heard what Bethany said. And I didn't know for sure that you heard me kill her. Wishful thinking, I know. I'm so sorry, Anna. I'm so sorry I won't be able to take care of you anymore, but you are going to be OK, you hear me?"

Anna shook her head. "Jackie, no, don't. You can't! They'll put you in prison! You can't! She gave you no choice! She deserves to die for what she did!"

Jackie shook her head. "No, she didn't, and I haven't slept a wink since. I lost it with her, but she didn't deserve to die. It was just like years of pent-up anger and fear came out of me and landed on her. I need to face the consequences, and I've already called the cops."

Gertrude stood up abruptly. "I've got to go."

No one even acknowledged her.

"Anna," Gertrude said. They heard sirens. Anna looked at her. "I was never here, all right? But I will be back. I will help you get out of here. OK? I've got very nice friends who will help you too." She looked at Jeb and Andrea. "I'll meet you guys at the car." Then she turned and opened the window.

"Gertrude!" Jeb cried.

Gertrude stuck one leg out the window. "Don't worry, I'm not jumping. There's a fire escape!" She pulled herself through the window, grateful that at least this time she wasn't being poked with a gun. When she'd extricated her whole body from the apartment, she stuck her head back in. Jeb and Andrea were already gone. The sisters were on the bed in a sad embrace. "Sorry to interrupt," Gertrude said, "but do either of you know anything about Gunslinger City?"

Anna ignored her, but Jackie said, "They were just in the news, weren't they?"

"Yes," Gertrude said impatiently, "but do you have any personal connection to them? Or do you know about any connections between them and Vacationland Development?" The sirens grew louder.

Jackie frowned. "Sorry, no, I don't."

"Okeydoke," Gertrude said. "Good luck, Jackie. And if you need one, I know a couple of really good lawyers."

Gertrude descended the fire escape a little faster than she'd intended. Gravity helped her more than she'd wanted it to. She stepped off the bottom of the steps just as two cop cars pulled up. She dove behind a dumpster to hide, and then peeked out to watch four men run into the building. *You don't need to run, you nincompoops. She's surrendering.* Gertrude stood up, straightened her wig, and headed toward Jeb's car.

25

Three days later, Gertrude's friend from church picked her up to take her to Anna's apartment.

"You've got the boxes, G?" she said, climbing into his truck.

"Yep, in the back."

"And anyone else going to help us?"

"Yes, Pastor Dan and Tiny are meeting us there."

"Did Pastor Dan talk to the developers?" Gertrude asked.

"Yep. They're going to have someone meet us there too."

"Great. And the paramedics are going to be there too."

"Good. Gertrude, I'm really proud of you. You're doing a good thing here."

"I know. I do good things sometimes, G."

When Gertrude and G got to Kennebec Street, two men were already cutting through the wall to make Anna's door bigger. Gertrude tapped one of them on the shoulder. He shut off his saw and looked at her expectantly. "Are you Vacationland Developers?" she asked.

"No, ma'am. Just a contractor."

"Fine," Gertrude said and walked past him into the apartment.

"What was all that about?" G asked from behind her.

Gertrude stopped, leaned on her walker, and looked back at him. "I don't know why, but there's just something fishy about that outfit. I thought this murder and the one up in Jackson were connected. I guess maybe they're not. But still, I don't trust these vacation people. I have no proof, or any clues even, but mark my words! *Eventually*, I'm going to catch them doing something wrong. They haven't seen the last of me!"

"Is that you, Gertrude?"

Gertrude recognized Jeb's voice.

"You sure do have a lot more friends than you used to," G remarked.

"Yes, well this gumshoe business has made me very popular," she said to G. Then she hollered, "Yes, it's me!"

Anna's eyes grew wide when she saw her. "Your hair!"

Not understanding, Gertrude reached one hand up to see what was wrong. Then she remembered. "Oh, yes, last time I was here, I was *in burrito*."

Anna frowned.

"So, how are you doing?" Gertrude asked.

"I'm freaking out."

"Don't freak out. Jeb here and Pastor Dan are going to make sure you have everything you need." She scooted closer to Anna and then lowered her voice. "I needed Pastor Dan's help once too."

Anna let out a deep breath.

"You look nice," Gertrude said.

"Thank you. Pastor Dan brought me a dress."

"It looks good. I like roomy clothes too."

"I see you have your walker now?" Anna said. "I thought you said you didn't need it."

Gertrude looked down at her walker and then pushed it over to G. "You're right. You walk out of here, and I'll walk out of here without my walker."

"I'm not sure how far she'll be able to walk, Gertrude," Jeb said.

Then Gertrude noticed the extra-large gurney beside him.

"All right. Well, you get wheeled out, and I'll walk beside you. How's that?"

Anna smiled through her fear. "Thanks, Gertrude."

"You betcha," Gertrude said. "It's all going to turn out spiffy. You'll see."

Large Print Books by Robin Merrill

Gertrude, Gumshoe Cozy Mystery Series
Introducing Gertrude, Gumshoe
Gertrude, Gumshoe: Murder at Goodwill
Gertrude, Gumshoe and the VardSale Villain
Gertrude, Gumshoe: Slam Is Murder
Gertrude, Gumshoe: Gunslinger City
Gertrude, Gumshoe and the Clearwater Curse

Wing and a Prayer Mysteries
The Whistle Blower
The Showstopper
The Pinch Runner

Shelter Trilogy (featuring Gertrude)
Shelter
Daniel
Revival

Piercehaven Trilogy
Piercehaven
Windmills
Trespass

Standalone Novella
Grace Space (the original Gertrude story)

*Robin Merrill also writes sweet romance as
Penelope Spark:*
The Billionaire's Cure
The Billionaire's Secret Shoes
The Billionaire's Blizzard
The Billionaire's Chauffeuress
The Billionaire's Christmas

Want the inside scoop?
Visit robinmerrill.com to join
Robin's Readers!

Made in the USA
Middletown, DE
27 August 2020